Contra Amatores Mundi

Graham Thomas Wilcox

Old Moon Publishing

CONTRA AMATORES MUNDI

Interior artworks by Mark Jarrell

An Old Moon Publishing book
Published by Old Moon Quarterly
Rochester, NY

First Old Moon Publishing Paperback Edition: 2024

979-8-9911399-1-5

www.oldmoonpublishing.com

Dedicated to Caitlyn Emily Wilcox

Contra Amatores Mundi

Love, that for very life shall not be sold,
Nor bought nor bound with iron nor with gold;
So strong that heaven, could love bid heaven farewell,
Would turn to fruitless and unflowering hell
—Swinburne, *Tristram of Lyonesse*

í

On a black ship within a blacker sea, Prospero and I slew the Knight of Foxes.

Before he died, he clasped us to him—tight as Cleopatra once clutched her final adders—and leapt.

As we fell, Walpurga reached out her hand (the one of flesh, not the one of bone), and though her fingers did not brush my plate, nor even my surcoat's edge, her eyes locked with mine and in their blaze I beheld something like the very pits of Hell, which ever burn, unacquainted with relief.

I vowed then, sure as the sword vows to its sheathing flesh, I would return to her.

But then the water gripped me and the Knight of Foxes breathed his last into my ear—laughing, by God and Saint Ottmer, *laughing*— and for a long time thereafter, I saw and knew nothing more (nor nothing less) than a knight's longing for his nun.

ii

𝔐𝔶 eyes opened upon a land beneath the sea.

Overhead, waves like jade born beneath the primeval night rippled for leagues upon leagues, unto the gates of dawn. I watched them a moment, for a man may treasure such sights but rarely. But then I recalled the black ship, and its blacker sea, and Walpurga.

Ah, Walpurga. Let me tell you of her. I shall be brief.

When our Order of the Dragon invested the keep of Havel Ironsides, and his cousins fell upon us with their retinues and their companies and encircled us in our camp (thus besieging we besiegers), Walpurga broke her bread and shared her water with our kenneled alaunts. This she did every day, even as her cheeks withered and her eyes sunk deep into the grave of her skull. Later, when Havel's castle burned, she tossed the bones of his wife and sons to those same hounds, and smiled.

Every evening before our slumber, she spoke to me of Eriugena and Plotinus and Ophidius and all the other heathen scholars of yore. In the morning, she would write down the prior night's thoughts in bloody ink upon a page of man-vellum. Often, she paused and licked the quill.

Her hair she wore long and unbraided and, like some great angel's wing, it blanketed my chest when she laid her head upon me. She smelled of wormwood and of lavender and (very faintly) of the smoke of pale Dis, where heretics burn. While she slept, her hands—the one of bone, and the one of flesh—ever sought my own. Always, they were cold.

All these memories, like Heaven's final glimpse ere the rebel angels fell, played through my mind as I sat upon that strand of clotted dark, and I know not how long I lost myself within them. But then I heard beyond me what I thought was some beast's hunting cry, clear and shrill as death bewinged. I rose to my knees.

Beside me lay the Knight of Foxes. His true name I leave unrecorded, as penance for his sins. I do not leave it unremembered though, for—no matter how he lived—he died a knight. With my palm, I closed his left eye (for his right I'd closed earlier with my axe), and then stood. My legs did not wobble, my breath did not rattle, and my vision did not swim. By such signs, a knight may know himself unwounded.

I stood upon a beach of white sand, its borders lapped by a sea still and black and in all other ways unlike its brother the sky, except in its vastness and its chill. Behind me landwards lay a scape of twisted rock, rising sharply into a pine-haunted forest and then sharper still into a massive hill. A tower toothed the top of that hill, and from its windows bright flames scorned the night.

A hand clanged onto my spaulder. I reached for my sword, and laughter boomed.

"How now, Hieronymus? You'd gift me your steel ere I even ask?"

Almost, I riposted with a laugh of my own. "I'd gift you an ell, brother, though you ask only an inch."

"That much? Only, I'd heard from a certain lady you offer rather the reverse."

Now I laughed in truth and, turning, beheld Prospero of Lucetti. A knight-paladin of our Order of the Dragon—in which office he matched myself—and I say this now, for he would not forgive me if I omitted it: violence never authored its writ upon a man more firmly than it did upon dread Prospero. Blood, fire and death had scrawled him all over, such that by the very ink of his eye and curl of his mouth, one branded him at once a son of Cain.

I looked him up then down, this knight, this fiend, this brother of mine. "You lack your heaume."

He bared his teeth, and the scars webbing his face puckered themselves into that rough and patchwork horror he mistook for a smile. "A vain bauble; I am the greater for its lack. My faith is my shield."

"Your face, perhaps."

Prospero slapped his cheeks. "That too. And you, brother? Are you hale?"

"As a hound."

"And twice as hairy, I darenot doubt."

"If only that much." I unbuckled my bascinet from my cuirass and thumped it into the sand. My arse followed presently.

Prospero, unperturbed and imperturbable in that manner unique to all elder killers of the earth, ambled over, plunked down next to me and harrumphed. "I care not for this place. It curdles my better humors. What say you?"

I considered his words. I say this now, and mark me, it shall not be repeated: my return to Walpurga's side was my utmost goal. Those of you who have—like Tristan—known your Iseult need no further explanation. To the rest of you I say only this: take up the sword and one day you too shall know.

That being said, I was no thaumaturge. Whatever gramary the Knight of Foxes had wielded in tombing us here alongside his corpse, I'd neither tongue nor touch for its counter. And yet, a man must act.

I waved a hand at the Knight of Foxes. "I daresay, yonder lich thundered us into one of Perdition's own oubliettes." I scowled. "I've no temper for respite. I reckon we best scarper, and swift."

"Whereto?"

"That, I cannot say."

"Alas, alack."

After that, a companionable, pondering silence. Time passed.

"Hark," I said at last, "an idea occurs."

Prospero grunted. "I reckoned I smelt something burning. What say you?"

I flashed him a grin and gestured again toward the Knight of Foxes. "Behold, augur, your canvas."

Again, Prospero crunched the map of his scars into one mountainous frown. "Must we?"

"We? Nay. Christ and His saints gifted me no talent for splanchomancy. This you know."

"Aye." Prospero puffed his cheeks and blew a long sigh. "A rude task, such butchery, I darenot deny it. Surely, you feel the same."

"We paint ourselves with claret to the elbow. What's another drop?"

Prospero frowned. "Might a man tire of the blood?"

"Does the drunkard tire of his wine?" I laughed, and then seeing he did not, halted.

"Aye, if the vintage turns vinegar."

"Eh?"

Prospero looked away from me, toward the churning sky. "Long have we fought, I say. Once, it all seemed such a glorious thing. The truth and the beauty of the truth of man against man, their blood their one and abiding wager. But now?" He spat upon the Knight of Foxes, and looked unimproved by the act. "It is not as I thought it might be."

I shall not renumber Prospero's virtues. But I will say this: always had I known him for a knight and the son of knights and a man stout as fired oak. Yet in that moment I looked on him and it seemed to me that if he were an oak, he was one withered and salted in its rooted earth, the bark of him sucked tight to his teeth, his cheekbones stark as heartwood bared beneath a knife, the boughs of his shoulders bent down as though they bore up above them all the rusting armors of the world.

I smiled at these thoughts and these sights as one must smile when befuddled by another man's melancholy. Prospero shuddered.

"Sheath your mirth, sir. Even a knight might stomach only so much horror." Groaning, he stood, loosed his misericorde, and marched towards the Knight of Foxes. In short order, he'd the man's breads slopped out upon the sand. He muttered over them an orison of our Order—*do ye indeed speak righteousness*, it began, *do ye judge uprightly, O ye sons of men?*—then sketched a sign upon the air. Petals of pale flame bloomed upon heart and liver and Prospero sucked deep the smoke therefrom and knelt, his eyes closed and fluttering beneath their lids as though sights unborn struggled therein.

A moment passed and he coughed and spat and, standing, staggered a step or three ere I caught him under his arms. "Peace, brother," I said, holding him up, "peace."

Prospero coughed again, then opened his eyes. "Yonder donjon," he said. "There our answers lie. So says the Lord."

I thumped Prospero on the back as one does when cheering a friend struck down upon the list. He spat again, wiped his mouth and grinned his grin of old, wide and toothsome.

"There will be blood," he said.

"We are knights of the Dragon. When is there not?"

"Aye, when indeed?" He wiped his misericorde clean and sheathed it. "We ought pray, I suppose. I wager we shall require all the intercession we might afford."

And so, kneeling beside the Knight of Foxes, we prayed to God and saint alike for the succor of their holy flame, their sacred void. In such moments, our Order's doctrine demands a knight hold within his inner sight the visage of Christ in all his glory, bright and smoking as iron quenched in gore. And yet, my mind's eye threw back naught but Walpurga's face: her cheeks, high and pale beneath their mantle of freckles; her hair, like copper a-flame beneath the westering sun; and her eyes, her eyes, which always cupped within them (like wine within the grail of night) the memory of bloody pasts, and the promise of bloodier futures.

ÍÍÍ

Bones salted the earth around the tower, some age-yellowed, others still red with the chrism of their birth. Harness and heraldry tangled each and every bone. By such signs, I knew them for the relics of knights. And indeed, a knight warded that tower's gate.

He was, I daresay, a queer sight. Mail shrouded him from heel to head in the old manner, and he wore a flare-topped heaume of ancient mien, such as one might glimpse illuminated on the pages of a crumbling psalter. His right hand clasped a shield, scarlet as sin and fashioned like a teardrop. His left held a morningstar; blood browned its haft and wet scalp furred its spikes. From high upon his thigh, where his mail hung loose and ragged, blood leaked. Upon the silver of his surcoat, three suns burned.

And he was, I aver, a spare three ells taller than any man I'd ever seen.

"Hail, sir," said Prospero as we approached. "We beckon your gate. Will you admit us?"

The giant-knight stirred, and it was like watching the earth rumble itself to wakefulness. His helm swept side to side, and the old abyss roiled within the bar of his visor, black and formless and yet not altogether inhuman.

"Hail daemons, and begone," he said. Thunder echoed in his voice, and it was not an unkind timbre.

I stepped forward. "We are no daemons. We are knights, sir."

The giant pointed his morningstar towards me, then Prospero, as though appointing us each to some fresh grave in hell. "Mark a man by the banner he flies, the King told me. 'The symbol reveals the man,' quoth he."

I looked at Prospero. His face revealed naught. I shrugged. "The dragon is a holy beast. Mightiest of all God's creatures. Thus do God's mightiest knights don its sigil."

Prospero made a noise. I frowned, but did not turn. The giant tipped back his heaume, as though drinking in the sight of us. "I see the blood upon you. Ricburgis. Gotland. Saletsa. Nicopolis."

At those names, I ground my teeth and said nothing. Prospero lifted his chin. "What know you of Nicopolis? Of Saletsa?"

"Blood," said the giant. "And flesh, monster. Blood and flesh."

"Not daemons," I said, "nor monsters. We are knights. We seek escape from this realm. Aid us, I ask you."

The giant shook his head. "Nay. It is not permitted. I ward the gate. I challenge the beasts. The King himself dubbed it so. That I remember. That, I remember." His shoulders slumped and a weariness freighted his words such as might afflict some future peak, tall and proud and ruinous upon a foreign plain, last of all its kith.

Prospero frowned and stared and for a time said nothing. No sorrow tugged down the corners of his mouth; no anger ruddied his cheeks. But confusion wrinkled his brow, the sort one glimpses on the faces of those grandfathers who search the visage of their sons, yet see only strangers. Recognizing in him those symptoms of our Order's perpetual affliction—praise be to Saint Dymphna, who wards us against such daemons—I muttered, in the theater of my mind, a dire curse.

Out loud, I whispered that prayer which begins, *And there met him out of the tombs a man of unclean spirit, and no man could bind him, no, not with chains.* And I touched Prospero on the shoulder as one touches a hound of sharp teeth and uncertain temper, for such was the gift and the curse of my years within our Order. One eye I kept upon the giant. One hand I held upon my sword.

Prospero looked at me and for a moment, that wrath and that fear peculiar to dotage clouded his eyes. My hand relaxed upon my sword—for the rested limb swings swiftest—but then he shook his head like a dog drenched by rain, and sighed and closed his eyes. When next they opened, they were clear and amber as the lifesblood of old trees.

"May there not be another way?" he said.

I nodded. "There may."

"You will not seek it."

I would like to say I thought about it. A wiser knight than I surely would have. But I did not.

"Behold, a white horse; and he that sat on him was called Faithful and True," I said. "And in righteousness he doth judge and make war."

For a moment, Prospero looked like he might argue or lapse again into his former fugue—indeed for a moment he resembled again that withered oak, the boughs of him trembling beneath a weight. But then the moment passed and he laughed and it was a wolf's mirth. "Judge and make war, aye. By the God, it is willed."

"Praise Him." I crossed myself and faced our giant and took my guard and from it saluted him with my sword, as man does to man. "We must make our road, sir."

The giant-knight returned my salute. "Aye, so I thought. Let it be a red one."

He lunged then, and by all the saints, he nearly had me. His first step brought him to me and his morningstar whistled down like the fist of God cleaving flat the natal earth. It jolted me to the dirt but my harness—thrice-sanctified upon the Altar of Night—held. He drew back for a second strike and Prospero was on him, the pike of his axe jabbing at knee and ankle and groin, a bittern cracking snails. The giant-knight swept out his shield and belted Prospero to his knees but then I stood and the prayers of our Order fell like cinders from my tongue—*For they have shed the blood of saints and prophets,* I sang, *and thou hast given them blood to drink; for they are worthy*—and my veins swelled and writhed like serpents and I hewed hard into that rent upon the giant's thew and blood gushed forth like water from Kadesh's stone and my gums ached at the sight of it and the giant roared and staggered and anviled me twice more ere I struck him once. Iron washed my tongue and darkness ate away the gray corners of my vision but I did not fall; I laughed aloud and it was my heart's own song.

Those of you who live by the sword shall know. For you unlucky souls who live elsewise, let me explain: battle is, like love, one of God's great gifts to Man. It is an ambrosia, for even those it slays, it immortalizes. Mark me: minstrels sing of no man who died upon his bed. But of Arthur, Hector, and fell Siegfried, no man may count the songs.

Again the giant hammered my helm and I spat blood and splintered his shield asunder with my riposte and then Prospero, rising like a pale wolf beneath his foe the bear, stalked widdershins behind the giant and lunged and his axe caught within its pike the glancing, lucent moon and then the giant howled and knelt upon the earth, his leg jousted to the marrow.

The giant swung once more and it was the flailing of Leviathan ere Michael fished him forth upon a lance of fire. I caught it with my sword but it smote me to my knees and numbed my arms to the shoulder and my sword shook and the giant drew back again, arm flung skyward, and it was then that Prospero thrust him beneath that upraised arm. The ring of steel bitten by steel, then the delicate noise of a fang on soft flesh—and Prospero danced backward, the giant's heartsblood uncorking itself in his wake. The giant sighed like a man betrayed and fell and did not move.

"I earned that bane," he said. "You are knights, I see it now. Come hither. I must tell you these things."

I looked at Prospero. Each of us bled, but it was that slow, dark blood shed only by those fed and bred upon the Dragon's sacrament, which clots quick and black as pinetar, and on its account I did not worry. A moment passed and Prospero stepped forward. I followed.

The giant unhelmed himself and fixed us with the sear of his gaze and by the God, I almost could not bear its heat.

"What you seek does not lie here. It comes only to those who might bear up its honor." Hoarse, his voice, and dry, as though all its smoothing waters leaked out with his lifesblood. "My mortality is no small victory. Yet, not enough. You must pursue. In pursuit, redemption. Do not falter. The unworthy falter. They bear their wounds eternal. They forget themselves. They dwell."

He shuddered then and his thigh trembled and bled anew. His throat gurgled and it was a beast's sound, low and urgent and unthinking in its pain. Bright blood bubbled from his mouth into the pale flag of his beard and his eyes rolled like skulls across a lichyard, white and red and white again.

He mastered himself. His eyes latched upon my own and he said to us, "gaze into my lights. I too once strode the path. Let this be my gift. The King would forswear me for it, but you are indeed my brothers. Some loyalties abide above all others. Look now and see the truths. Aye, and the lies."

I did not move, but Prospero stepped forward without hesitation. Shamed, I followed likewise. I looked into the giant's eyes, *and*—

—*upon* a black ship within a blacker sea, Walpurga fought a knight.

Holy fire wreathed her hands. At her chanted word it crawled forth over hand and air towards her foe and, within a crow's breath, black flame embraced the knight, its many tongues licking his greaves, his fauld, his heaume. He bowed beneath their ardor, a Roland before his Aude.

But then he rose, and his surcoat sloughed from his breastplate like skin off a snake and his sword he raised above his head, and when it fell, Walpurga fell with it *and*—

—*within* a nun's cell, spare of wealth and warmth alike, Walpurga raised a corpse. By its head, a red candle guttered. Salt etched the secret names of God and devil alike upon the stone between lich and lady.

Walpurga's mouth moved and the corpse juddered, one arm twitching, then another. Finally, it sat up and its mouth flapped open and graveworms, round and ripe as a baby's fingers, flopped from its tongue. For a long time the corpse spoke, but its voice was like the murmur of a child, and though I heard, I did not understand *and*—

—*atop* a bed reclined Walpurga, naked. A man lolled beside her. He too was *naked*—

—*and* I stepped back from the giant. My hands shook, so I clasped them behind my back. Prospero was kneeling, which I did not mark at the time but later thought strange, for never had I seen him kneel before any man or daemon but the Lord. He looked at me and stood and I stepped away. Before either of us might speak, the giant convulsed again. His belly rippled, then his chest, then his throat, as though he cocooned some kicking thing, eager for its own unveiling.

And indeed in the next moment his mouth gaped wide and wide and wider yet until it unseamed itself by its roots in a welter of blood and tooth and bone and a serpent's head, slick with the gore of its womb, nosed through that ruptured mass. Yet a serpent's body did not follow. I glimpsed spotted fur, heard the clatter of hooves and then the serpent—the beast—was gone, bounding away into the trackless night.

iv

Prospero started after it. I arrested his advance with a hand upon his cuirass. He rounded on me, and in his eyes a red joy burned.

"Unhand me, man. We must pursue. By the God, did you not see?"

"By the devil, I saw, and all too much." I turned and spat upon the giant's corpse. "Windows into some enchanter's calumnies, I wager."

The bile of my voice varnished away some of Prospero's fervor. His brow furrowed. "What did you see?"

I told him, and his brow did not unwrinkle.

"That is not what I saw."

"Then imagine me your palimpsest, sir."

"Eh?"

"Fill me in, sluggard."

"I saw a tower upon a hill and from it great wafts of fire slashed away the nightly brume. The sky cleared and before the tower stood that beast. A loathsome creature but lovely in its loathsomeness, like a lance of Turks drawn up upon a field beneath the summer's sun, daring you to charge. I heard no voice, you understand, but it was as if I did and it said: *here, you must conquer.*"

"That is all?"

Prospero shifted from foot to foot, skittery as an alaunt before the hare. "I felt as though I stood upon the tourney-field, champion of all men but one. And I remembered, in that moment, the man I once was, though I had not known I had forgotten it—nor even that such a forgetting was possible. And he, that one beast, stood before me and beckoned, and all the eyes of all the kings of the world pinned themselves upon me, waiting for my spur, my cry."

I understood him. I was a knight of the Dragon; how could I not? Yet when I closed my eyes, I saw again Walpurga in her extremity, in her nudity.

"Walpurga," I said, and nothing more. Prospero's eyes flickered. His jaw worked.

"She is just a woman," he said at last. "What else did you expect?" Then he thumped a hand against my back and smiled. "Come, Hieronymus. It is a *quest*, by Christ and all His saints. You heard yon giant. We shall not dwell. It is as you said. We are knights, man. Knights!"

Without awaiting my response, he turned and strode away. At first I thought he made for the tower's gate but when I looked, I saw we now stood no nearer the tower than when we'd first awoken upon the shore. In the distance now it loomed, as though speared into the very horizon by the Morningstar's hand, one last defiance against bleak Heaven's folly.

I watched Prospero walk towards it for a time, a man alone. He allowed himself no backward glance.

I followed him. How could I not? I would be as he was—-and indeed, had I not once been worse?—were it not for Walpurga, or for this chronicle, which I began only at her insistence. So aye, I followed him.

But first, I cut the giant's eye from its socket. It was like no eye I'd ever seen, hard and smooth, more like glass than flesh. Soon, it jounced upon my belt. It weighed heavy as a man's unboiled skull.

vi

The Tower was our lodestar. Across a black realm, we chased it.

The first week, Prospero and I walked and fought and bled and slew. We tracked the Beast by its sign and spoor. We listened by night to its howl and by day to the drum of its tread, like thunder on the steppe. We glimpsed it in its terror and its splendor—the night-soaked sheen of its scales, the tawny gold of its fur, jewelled here and there with black spots like eyes—as it stood like a stag in summer, proud upon the horizon. But always it fled at our approach.

We japed at our work—Prospero knew a ribaud's share of dirty jokes, as do all Italians—and we argued the merits of this helm or that blade (Prospero favored more open helms, I more closed). Manserpents, like statues carved in miniature of the Beast, dogged our heels. We skinned them and cloaked ourselves in their dripping hides. We necklaced ourselves in their teeth and their ears, that we might tally the score of our battles. We spitted their heads in palisade about our camp, and smiled. Prospero rose every morn a man renewed by the prior day's blood, a blade insatiable held high against the dawn. I would have joined him in this resurrected vigor, I think, but for our nights. I stood every wolfing hour's watch and there perhaps dwelt my true reason for accompanying Prospero—though I cannot say if that is so, or if it is my own mind's teeth spitting my shame back at me.

Regardless: the night, and its watches. I shall begin with the first of them, for in its mould I cast its future fellows. We'd walked long and far that day after the giant's death, and slain already the first of the manserpents, who sprang upon us from some trees like crows scattered off a body. A hard fight. In its aftermath, we prayed above their corpses, their blood splashed over us like oil on the brows of kings new-crowned, our own bodies marked by the stigmata of our work.

It is here I must say something of those hurts a knight bears, for they are the foremost coin paid him by his vocation; how he spends them defines something of his soul. Some knights, subscribing to that Christian virtue we name charity, view each wound thus paid as a debt they must avenge. Others view them less as debts and more as shames, but those shames such as children find, which become lessons treasured, yet despised. For my own humor, I possessed something of the latter—and something rather more of the former. But there are other knights who think elsewise. For them, each wound earned in battle made them neither debtor nor student, but rather promoted them to something like that station occupied by the sainted Sebastian, their every cut transubstantiated to one more arrow thrust through a blessed flesh, each shaft a new and heady martyrdom, worthy by its bite alone. An alluring thought, perhaps. Yet that was not Prospero's way, nor my own. Or rather, it had not been.

But that night, Prospero sat beside our fire and marveled like a squire hitherto unblooded at his each and every wound. He pointed them out to me, his smile hooked wide by the flicker of the flame: here a sword blow, there a mace strike, each spot of blood (by the glow of his eyes and the tenor of his voice) a gift.

"A wondrous fray," he said, again and again. "A wondrous fray."

So he spoke until slumber took him. I begrudged him nothing of his wonder—and would not begrudge him his later vigors, for all I lacked them. There had been other nights, yea and days as well, where my own enthusiasms must surely have outshone his own, and mayhaps on those days Prospero wore his patience like a shirt of hair, and smiled. A knightly deed if so, and one all men must someday practice, if men they be.

Yet, night so often breeds in a man that black bile we call melancholy, and no night moreso than one spent alone. Aye, alone I say, for though Prospero slept not three strides distant, I—who had so often bedded down besides Walpurga—felt myself now orphaned by her absence. I could not sleep, for it was my watch, yet above all else I desired sleep and the oblivion it grants, and few tortures vex a man more than to lust for abolition from the self, but to be by his own duty denied.

Perhaps then, what happened next was inevitable. I write that, and it is a heresy, for we knights of the Dragon—alone of all men living—choose. Such is the liberty afforded us by our imitation of that arch-knight Christ, and His saints. To us, no defeat is inevitable. So reads our catechism.

I offer this in my defense, and perhaps (like many defenses) it must only prove my guilt. But I am a knight sworn to his truth, and so a truth I offer. I begin with this: a knight on watch must keep his eyes peeled for his foe. Which is to say, he must remain alert and untroubled—a man wired unblinking to his vigilance shall soon find, like the swordsman who whiteknuckles his hilt, that he strains himself to impotence. So, some idle thought is no great sin; indeed, it can be (in its right proportion) a boon. But my thoughts that night turned ever and anon towards Walpurga—or rather, her deeds and fates unveiled to me by the giant's eyes. They tormented me, the memory of those visions, such that I knew some inkling of the drunkard's need for his drink, which consumes within him for its fuel the bibulous cheer it creates, leaving behind only that ash which is his sorrow. But like the drunkard, I thought perhaps some tipple from that imperfect fount might balm me against its burn (and so keep me fresher for my watch). And too, had the giant's eye not revealed to us some picture of our fate, some vision of worlds other than this one into which fate thrust us? Thus, I reasoned (in much that same fashion as many men reason to their wineskins) that a glimpse into the mirror of that giant's eye might reveal to me some glimpse of Walpurga, some clue of our escape from this realm, some insight into how Prospero's mad hunt furthered my own quest (for I knew, were I to escape this strange land, I might need his sword-arm). It is an unchivalrous thought, that last, for a man should aid his brother free of all self-interest. Yet is it not unchivalrous to lie as well? To the self, even if to no other?

Regardless, having marshaled my reasons and judged them sound (said Michael to the Morningstar), I set my back to Prospero and our fire, unhasped the giant's eye from my belt and gazed into it, feeling rather ridiculous, a charlatan staring portents into his quartzine orb.

And at first, the eye reflected naught but that grand and unornamented abyss which is the father of Night and of the Sea and of all the other dark spaces of the world (excepting Man, and his heart). Yet just as I prepared to set it down, a faint light glimmered therein like a candle lit upon the deep, and it bloomed brighter and by this coal I—

—saw Walpurga, bent over a desk piled high with books and scrolls and those rune-marked skulls of necromancers, who by the new moon speak Hell's own secrets. The red banner of her hair curled unwashed around her head and tears gathered unshed in the corners of her eyes. At her left hand, a black candle flickered.

"The barrier," she read aloud, "shall not be broken, but by two reagents: a death undeserved, or a love unbroken."

She heaved shut the tome whence she'd rattled off her words and stared for a time into that dark beyond her candle's light. Then she raised her hand and with its ungloved bone snuffed the candle, *and—*

—I saw a throne carved in the shape of knights knelt and bloodied beneath an altar. Before it bowed Walpurga, posed like one awaiting a formal dialogue, or an execution. Upon the stoneshod ground beneath her, three tools of power lay: an axe, cleft in twain; a chalice, bronzed and bloodstained; a book, blackbound and gilt-lettered.

"No," said the woman sat upon the throne, ere Walpurga's head raised again. This woman enthroned was decked, like Walpurga, in a nun's habit, the badge of our Order blazoned on her breast (*gules, a cross fleury fitchy sable inflamed or*) and her face was a saint-queen's ageless mask, unlined by fear, pity or mercy.

"Beloved mother," said Walpurga, "I believe there exists a gramary which might cure our Order of this sorrow inflicted upon it by perfidious chance."

"I've no doubt your insight cleaves deep as ever, O daughter of Christ. But I admit, I am unacquainted with this stony sorrow upon which you grind its edge. Introduce us, I pray, lest I—for sake of ignorance—nick myself upon its unseen point."

Walpurga paused a moment. "I speak of our dear brothers, Hieronymus of Tsorn and Prospero of Lucetti, who pagan mischief warlocked into that higher realm whose gate was, notwithstanding our communion with its saints, hitherto thought impermeable. As I said, I believe—"

The mother-superior held up one hand. Walpurga's mouth clicked shut. "Their death is no sorrow. Is martyrdom not the joy above all joys?"

Walpurga's brow furrowed. She nodded. "Praise be to God." She raised one finger. "Yet I've great reason to believe they are not martyred, merely whisked off into one of those realms parallaxed from our own. If you recall your Plotinus, or even our own Gospel of Saint George—"

"I recall them well, Walpurga of Wildgraf." Ice tipped the mother-superior's voice, fit to chill the sun itself to premature night. "If the brothers in question are not martyred, then that is indeed a sorrow. It would spare them the shame of confinement to the ranks of our Eldest Brethren. A fate which loomed, you must agree, on their horizons. The signs were plain as the stars, and nearer too."

A shadow darkened Walpurga's face, like unto that darkness which shades the knight's helm ere his lance lowers. "Regretfully, I must admit my dissent."

The mother-superior clicked her tongue. "I have read the reports of the blackfriars. Their judgment was clear. Our esteemed and martyred brothers wrote their decline in the blood of Ricburgis' Land, and Saletsa green. There were excesses." She crossed herself. "May God judge them with the mercy they themselves forsook."

"Never would I accuse Saint Dominic's sons of harboring false hearts. Nor would I accuse them of bearing witness against our brethren, especially not in those instances wherein they themselves might be culpable." Walpurga sighed. "And, yet."

"And yet, the peasants near Saletsa say they still plow up skulls, I am told. Small ones, some of them."

"Peasants say many things."

"As do burghers sworn to the Hansa. And priests reporting to the Bishop of Riga—who remains, I need not remind you, no friend of ours. He knows some, and suspects more. We are not yet so mighty that we may defy the world alone, no matter what our honored brothers say." The mother-superior shook her head. "I sympathize, Walpurga, truly. A woman may love a hound, even as his sight fades and his teeth dull. But when he begins snapping at her guests, she knows what she must do to protect her name, and the honor of her house."

"It seems to me that a woman might hear of a man bitten, and yet check her kennel for his blood ere she stoves the hound's head." Walpurga smoothed her habit. "Nevertheless, my method, which I've demonstrated these past years and recounted before this very throne, surely revealed itself as a fit prophylactic— if not, in fundamental truth, a cure—to our brothers and their affliction."

The mother-superior's eyes flashed. "By the bones of Mother Mary, speak plainly child. Sauce me not with your pretensions towards study. We both know what fires compel you in this matter."

Walpurga raised one brow. "If aught governs my will, I name it sacred knowledge, mother-superior, and nothing more. Let me trim back the fat from my tongue, and say only this: if our brothers indeed still count themselves among the living, then study of their demeanors when shorn of my method must surely shed more light upon its efficacy. And if we may, in our search for them, discover reliable means of ingress into those realms through which they now meander, it must surely enlighten us towards a method of communion with both saint and devil which might outstrip our present—"

The mother-superior held up her hand. "If, if, if. Let the dead lie dead, sister. Your work upon them was admirable. Never did they think—well, it need not be said. You know, and we praise you for it. Yet if you pursue this matter, then…" Her hand lowered. "Such is the Word. Glory be to God."

Walpurga waited a breath. Then, she bowed lower. "Your will be done, mother-superior."

She straightened and smoothed again the rumpled skirts of her habit and her eyes were dry, *and*—

—*I* saw Walpurga straddle-legged atop a destrier, her head hooded, her face below its edge grim and lonesome and beautiful. A night-forest encompassed her, black and verdant as the Garden ere God kindled His sun. From her saddle, three things hung: axe, chalice, tome. Halting upon a hill, bald at its crown of oak and elm and grass alike, she dismounted. The tome she opened upon her lap; the chalice she stood upright before her; and with the axe, its sundered haft rough within her bone-bright palm, she slashed her arm above her hand of flesh. She spoke aloud words of Greek and words of Latin. She proclaimed the blood was the life; love was eternal; perdition's everlasting warmth was a small price to pay ere she saw again the face of he she loved more than sweet Gnosis itself. Thunder crashed, unheralded by the gaudy tongue of its father the lightning, and to the moon she raised her gory arm and from her wound, its lips flapagate like that portal whence all men enter this world, blood like tears flowed up and up and up. And the moon blacked its beacon, *and*—

—*I* saw a heretic's tree, whose leaves are flame and whose seed is ash, and there, nailed upon its bole, crowned in bitter smoke, wailed Walpurga—

—*and* I jolted away from the eye as though jousted in my traces by Gawain himself. My heart trebled its own beat. The wound in my chest unstitched itself and wept anew.

Dawn arrived and we arose and followed the Tower. The sun, a skull wigged bloody by the scalper's knife, leaked upon us day and night and day again till all melted into one general twilight unadulterated by the touch of God, man or angel. We walked on.

vii

It is the custom of our knights when on campaign to pray each morning and each night. But our prayers are not the prayers of lesser men.

Of course we speak aloud the Latin in its proper forms, for few know better than we the power of the tongue and its mastery over flesh. But the true mystery of our Order lies in that art called *imitatio*. Boethius said that he who impales his heart most firmly to the Christ's will is a man most free, for the Christ (being the font of all Goodness and Perfection) is himself the very essence of Freedom (which is, as even the smallest bairn can tell, the highest of all virtues). And, as D'Aquino said, imitation of Christ is how man must demonstrate his commitment to His will. Thus, as Christ is the arch-knight, perfect by his nature in the sweep of his blade and the hammer of his hew, so must we knights endeavor to achieve that selfsame perfection. Therefore, our prayer is war.

I say this all so you will know what regimen Prospero and I observed upon our hunt, at least on those days uninterrupted by hallowed battle. We swaggered staves, hurled stones, leapt high and ran long, and in all other ways exercised our flesh so that, when the moment arrived, we did not shame our swords (and thus, our God).

Often, such prayers tax soul and flesh alike. Any man among you who has lived, even for a week, the life of arms must know the truth of what I speak. We knights martyr ourselves upon the altar of chivalry. And like all martyrs, we must endure our Gethsemanes.

Yet I confess, there is much beauty and pleasure in such a life. Once, I upbucketed a stone from the earth which matched my own weight in harness, and hurled it three man-lengths hence. Many times have I woken ere the sun blazes the world to life and seen—by the light of old stars—my own blood flowing, and known it for a beauty. My flesh knits its own wounds, as if kin to the emberish salamander; my sword chews iron as the fang of a wolf chews lambflesh; my lance skewers the cold-drake's flesh when it heaves, dreadful dripping, from its chill and salted lair. No man moves me, if I wish not to be moved. Hosanna to God in the highest.

All this I write not as the common man might boast, but as the penitent who, with his own tongue, indicts himself. To pray as I have prayed, a man must focus. He must commit. From this, all truth is born. The God is One—so must we, his chosen knights, be likewise union in our efforts and our deeds.

Prospero exemplared this fact. He prayed day and night upon our hunt. Sweat wept from him in its streams, its rivers. His hands bled, his flesh bruised, but the rumble of his laugh and the whisper of his chant and the crosshatched horror of his smile proclaimed his virtue, impervious as Siegfried's hide. If I say I matched him, I would brand myself a liar. Yet, if his ardor for the life chivalric outshone (in that moment) my own, it was in that manner the sun outshines the moon—brightly so, but with, perhaps, some less beauty.

I tell you this that you might know me for no show-braggart or flabbermouth. All knights, no matter how holy, require as refreshment that one and unalienable balm of the mortal mind: that slicéd death we name sleep. Without it, even men sharpened by our Order's iron virtue shall, in time, blunt. And so, knowing this, our Order dictates in its Rule that proper sleep *must* be taken whenever possible, else we distemper from ourselves our most sacred edge. Prospero observed this precept of our Rule with what I might describe, in terms most charitable, as thunderous aplomb.

But I, burdened now with my giant's eye, absolved myself of the necessity of sleep. In its place, I sought in that orb each night one more sight, one more glance, one more glimpse of my Walpurga.

If Prospero noted by dawn the half-lidded stupor of my eyes, or observed by dusk the sleepless addle of my limbs, he did not say. But then, he was a man married to his hunt. Every spare moment we possessed undevoted to our prayer or our battles, he devoted to cutting for sign, scraping for trails, at times snuffling the earth like an alaunt, and other times evoking with his art some other, more esoteric, divinations.

The third week of our hunt, this last paid its debt. Within the heart of a forest damp and dark and unlike in many ways its brethren in the world above, Prospero spoke words of fire over the viscera of a squamous thing, and the whispers of daemons directed our steps thence. It spoke of mountains upthrust against the heavens, and bogs where witchlights winked, and the great vast forest where shadows— like lovers—lay.

We were undeterred. The Tower grew nearer every morn, more distant every night (which we judged now only by our wakings and our slumbers), until one day in a forest of pine, we heard a wolf mourning the absence of its moon. Our ears pricked up.

We looked and beheld again the Tower and Prospero roared his triumph, for it stood nearer to us than ever it had since the giant's death. But then we heard the cry of the Beast, which is a serpent's hiss and a leopard's yowl, and Prospero roared again and we took our guards. My blade I held upon my shoulder in the Guard of the Lady and Prospero held his axe low in the Boar's Tooth. A breath passed, and another, and another yet, and overhead the sky ceased its rippling as though its own passengers, holding fast their breath, leaned forth in anticipation of blood. And just when it seemed as though the night might give way beneath its own weight, the Beast unfolded itself from between those two trees nearest us.

I shall speak little of the battle, for little there is to say. We hemmed the Beast in close: it wore the hooves of a hind upon the trunk of a leopard, and its head was indeed a serpent's head and it was swifter than the sum of its mismatched quarters. Prospero drew first blood and it hissed and bit and darted here then there like a falcon bating. I struck for its rear legs, that we might hamstring it and finish it at our leisure. But perhaps my sleepless nights had bled from me some greater portion of my prowess than I suspected, for I fumbled my approach and the Beast, evading my blow, struck me down. Its teeth gouged through my plate and pain curdled my stomach and I cried aloud as it flung me down and crouched above me. In doing so, it bared its back to Prospero—and I saw that were he to strike, he might cleave it to its doom. But not before it slew me.

He did not hesitate. It reared back and struck and Prospero's axe was there, warding its fangs from my neck. It hissed and roared and stomped a dent into his cuirass and he fell. Then it turned and bounded back, back into the night. With it faded the Tower.

Afterwards, staring into the dark, my shame like blood splashed across my face and my voice gravelled raw by choler, I said to

Prospero (who stood unsmiling above me), "what devil cursed us with such a foe?"

Hearing my question, he stroked his beard and thumbed his axe and rattled the skulls chained like beads along his belt and muttered beneath his breath in the Latin tongue and for a moment I feared I'd again awoken within him the affliction of our Order. But then laughter roared up from his belly and he punched my arm and looked at me as if he spoke truths known to all men. "Do you not jest? A knight is only so worthy as his foes. Man needs his adversary. What would Christ Morningstar be without the Sainted Michael?"

Still laughing, he walked away, eyes set already upon the trail ahead. His words resounded, stirring within me some unnamed, unnameable yearning: perhaps that which swords feel for their oiling blood, or destriers for their spur and charge upon the wide clear plain. I felt in that moment I could have cut that yearning from my veins and sluiced it wholesale into a biliary flask, that I might sup upon it time and again to remind myself of who I was, of who I am. I swore, by God and all his saints, I would disdain the giant's eye and the false succor of its visions, and by my untruncated slumber renew myself for the morning's prayer, the morrow's hunt.

And like so many oaths birthed in the aftermath of a man's downfall, its life was an autumn flower: withered ere the first snows mantled it. That very night, while Prospero (seeking no doubt to aid my sleep) stood both my watch and his own, I sconced myself in those shadows beyond the nightfire's glare, drew forth again the giant's eye, *and*—

—*saw* pale mountains. Across them rode Walpurga atop an ebon steed, leading knights. Gore matted those rags which were her dress. Rust mossed the knights' armor. None wore the crimson of the

Order. They rode in column; some tottered in their saddles. Time passed, and one among their number jested with his fellows in the manner of fighting men the world over. Others joined him. Soon, their laughter fired the air. But Walpurga did not sway. She did not jest. She did not laugh. She sat tall in her saddle like a knight—and indeed, she rode a knight's destrier—and in the clench of her jaw, the furrow of her brow, one might have read a will so obdurate, so absolute, as to frighten all humor out of fashion.

Beside her rode a woman. She wore a plain dress, and beneath her hawk's nose a small mouth curled. She rode sidesaddle. Her eyes twinkled like a fox.

"Is this where we shall find the gate? Will we see the man-headed lions which prowl its utter edge?"

Walpurga shrugged. She wore a thin shift, ragged at the edges, a shroud nibbled by ghouls. The chill stained blue the fullness of her lips. Her teeth chattered. "Perhaps. The art is not exact."

Silence, but for the speech of knights, the clomp of hooves on earth, the distant clarion of a hawk seeking flesh. The woman fingered a cross at her neck. For a time, she hummed beneath her breath the bars of an old song, over and again. The sun dipped, and painted their shadows longer yet against the canvas of the world.

"Love," the woman said, and her mouth worked, swilling the word like verjuice about her tongue. "It is a paper pedestal, I think. Easy to gaud, but liable to wilt when stepped upon."

Here she paused, waiting in that manner adopted by scholastics engaged in a formal dialogue. Walpurga looked at her, then away. She said nothing, and for a time they rode through the mountains unaccompanied by the music of their speech, and the stones themselves of that land fraught and leprous beneath their steeds, as though slopped with ash born of a flame old and subterrene, and the hooves of the horses pranced sideways over them, and along their path twisted upthrust from the earth the black trunks of trees like beggar's hairs. A world sparse and foul and lesser than its past.

"I tender my apologies," the woman said at last, "that was an ill essay." When Walpurga persisted in her silence, the woman swallowed. "What I meant to say, is that I profess myself your most forthright admirer."

Walpurga looked at her again, her eyes bladed side-long.

The woman blushed. "Of your scholarship, I mean to say. It is an inspiration."

"Thank you."

A smile brightened the woman's face. "You're quite welcome. That is why I mention love. I agree with your study of it. What the mother-superior and the other sisters say of you is—Blessed Virgin forgive me—wrongheaded."

"Indeed." Now the path widened and they rode through columns of stone heaped by the hands of Romans, or by Vlachs, or perhaps by bloodlines of antediluvian and degenerate pedigree, these old rocks leaning against the air like dotards disheveled and unmortared from their founding youth. In the alcoves gutted from their stomachs rested skulls, papery and jawless, their plates unjoined at the apex, inheritors of a void unpromised by their fathers, scions of fever among whom rats kept house. The woman stooped and swept up a skull as she rode by, a three-eyed and behorned artifact, fragile in the cup of her hands as virtue itself. She turned it over. She sniffed.

"The Great Mortality is half a century past, by God. Yet still its taint fallows even these rocks."

Walpurga glanced up at that guttered coal which was their sun. "Why should it not?"

She clapped her hands together, the slap of one against the other echoing dull amid the columns, bounding and rebounding, those stones so long mute given again a voice, and they too now ignorant of their past, whether they be the ribs of Old Rome or marrow of a more recent vintage, and among them now hunched Walpurga, statued black against the horizon, a tatterdemalion caryatid thresholded over Limbo.

Behind her, the knights ceased their chatter. Lances clattered onto spaulders; swords whispered free of their scabbards. Walpurga dismounted Iscariot. She stroked his muzzle and whispered in his ear and fed him a wrinkled apple. She pulled from his saddlebag a pouch of salt, and scattered its contents in a circle upon the ground.

The woman dismounted, dropped the skull and, stepping over its shards, followed Walpurga. "Is it here?"

An axe joined the salt. Then, a chalice. Walpurga did not look up from her work. "It is easier with two."

The woman dismounted. She knelt down beside Walpurga. They sat very near the mountain's lip—an ell beyond their knees yawned the maw of the world, toothed in stone and darkness, blacker than the dimming sky above as hell is (at its ultimate lake) blacker than all the cloistered heavens.

"Closer," said Walpurga. The woman hesitated, eying the abyss. Walpurga's laughter sparkled forth like rain upon a meadow. "I do not bite. More than I may say for young Iscariot, mind you, so take care." The woman shuffled nearer, avoiding the destrier's head. Walpurga rested a hand upon her shoulder and smiled. "Love, sister. Disgorge me more of my opinion on the matter, if you will. For a scholar to hear another ape her words, it is the very meat and myrrh of the world. I shall have more of it."

The woman traced the rim of the chalice with her finger. "We will fill this with—"

"Ah, the laborer is worthy of her hire. Yes, the blessed bile. No, not that flask, the other one. Correct. In a moment, though. My doctrine of love, if you please."

The woman glanced towards the wilting sun. "You are certain we shall find the gate here?"

Walpurga looked down at her hands. Then, reaching across the circle of salt, she laced her fingers around the woman's neck. They sat very near the abyss, and night swallowed the horizon.

It was in those moments, just before all light fled the mountains, that the first manticore flew forth from its shaded crag. It landed, claws splayed, upon Walpurga's *steed*—

—*and* at a crossroads, Walpurga halted. Her habit hung from her in its loops and strips like the many skins of that immortal serpent whose slither first forecast Man's downfall. Dust skirled across her path and she shut her eyes against its sting and when again she opened them, three men beheld her.

"By the pricking of my thumbs," the first man said. He was stooped low as Atlas by the years piled atop his shoulders, his flesh wattled into that soft and uniform age which presages the liquescent grave, his hair a straggle of gray string. He leered as he spoke.

"Away, corpse," said Walpurga. She leaned on a staff as if beset by an infirmity beyond her smooth and springling years. But in her eyes, Chaos and old Night mingled.

"The villainies of your nature," said the second man, "seduce us out from our appointed hovels." A veteran's gut paunched his waist. A blackfriar's robe, pallored gray by ash and flour and the mold of tombs, draped him. His ragged tonsure, his scrape-stubble beard, his

Mammon grin—the stigmata of the universal uncle, swaying and sweating, winesot wisdom dripping from his lips.

"Sirrah," Walpurga said, "gnat me not with this chatter. Else you shall, like the mayfly, heat yourself once by this beacon's flame, yet be by it for your whole life warmed." She snapped her fingers, and sparks like stars birthed, then died. A nail on her right hand blackened, wrinkled and peeled off from her finger, wafting bloody to the earth, a leaf blown from a tree long dead.

"You seek," said the third man, "that Vulgar Venus which flouts the heavened soul." Youth bulked him. Hair like flax new-threshed thatched his head. Hose hugged his thews. Nails, red and hot, pierced his eyes. They waggled like terrier tails when he spoke.

Walpurga cowered not one step back—yet nor flamed she one step forward. She shuttered her eyes and rubbed with her dirt-grimed fleshling hand the dappled saddle of her nose. "To which corner of Hell has my quest not been by black wings flown?"

"To none," said the first.

"And to all," said the third.

"Your Order abandons you," said the second, stroking with one inky finger the thick tail of his beard. "They deny your love. They refuse you the shelter of their shields, the luxury of their lances."

Walpurga gnawed her lower lip. She leaned against her staff. She shuddered; she coughed. "I confess, I am vexed," she said. "I seek a land beneath the sea. I seek a knight."

"We can deliver you hence," said the three, each in echo of each.

Walpurga sighed. Her eyes glittered. "By what price?"

The first man threw back his rags. The second man heaved up his robe and his pale paunch. The third man stepped forward and it was as if the night itself vapored away his garments. His hand he held betwixt his legs, *and*—

—*I* beheld a vast cathedral, arched and spired and carved all over in minute tales of red death, of weird slaughter. Snow and ice cloaked it and above its gable the dark Moon bladed the clouds asunder and from their ruin haloed the cathedral's gates in her pale fire. And the gates opened and there upon their threshold reclined Walpurga.

Yet she was not that woman whom I remembered and loved but rather some titan twin, draped like a princess of dead Camelot in an argent robe, her body grown vast as the mountains, her breasts like battering rams, her thighs like towers, a crescent of smile riving bright her mouth, wide and terrible as the moon. Even so, I reached out to her with unreserved unhesitant passion and my own hand was a goliath's paw.

But when my hand met her flesh, it was as though I grappled with moonbeams and stardusts, my fingers groping through her and around her, yet never on her. And before I might say aught else, before I might clasp to myself that maddening light and force it carnal by will and kiss alone, Walpurga shimmered.

Shimmered and burst into a thousand thousand gilded petals, each flaring brief and halfborn as the thoughts of fools. Above me the hateful sun unsheathed his dread sword the horizon, routing from the sky Queen Night and bleeding red her purpled flesh and it was day *and*—

—*I* saw a room. Tapestries curtained its walls and the warm light of many candles buttered it smooth, so that the woman who sat within its round seemed herself something baked by the hearth of the world, fresh and soft and smiling. She sat upon a chair of red wood and leather and at first I thought she wrote, for her hands moved and her back bent, but I was mistaken. She straightened and rubbed her neck with her left hand (gloved in grey chamois) and I saw the sewing needle wink like a secret eye in her right hand. Then, she bent again and stitched her attention to her cloth. The winter of her years had dashed white the cinnamon of her hair, and the curve of her breasts and the fullness of her hip were fuller yet beneath the pale dress she wore and the candles by their flicker revealed new wrinkles amid the speckled ivory of her cheeks. But even so, she was Walpurga. And though no high drama accosted her here, she fettered my eyes as ever she once had (and as she always would). The candles danced and her hands rose and fell with a motion much like the waves under which I now walked and fought and slew, and she smiled as she worked, and hummed betimes such songs as women sing to themselves when no men are near. But then the door behind her creaked open and the child entered, weeping.

Walpurga stood and turned, smooth as a cat rising before its pounce (smooth, indeed, as rose a younger Walpurga in dead Carpathia on that night when she first plighted to me her troth, just before the Bey and his sipahis found us). Setting down her needle and her cloth, she scooped the child and kissed her and whispered in her ear words I could not hear, and rocked her. The girl buried her head in her mother's shoulder—for the red of her hair and the spotting of her face foretold her maternity, even if Walpurga's cuddling of her had not—and she trembled as I'd seen the whelps in our kennels tremble against their dames when thunder smote the night and lightning hammered day from gentle dark. They stayed that way for quite some time, mother and daughter, and other than Walpurga's initial whispers they spoke no words. Walpurga swayed and hummed now a different tune, a lullaby old when our fathers' fathers were young, and though our daughter's tears (for her eyes, I had seen, were blue as my own) darkened a patch of her dress, that darkness ceased growing after a time, even as the candles dimmed.

If you read this account, then you are (I darenot doubt) sworn in some fashion to our Order. If that is so, then you shall know the doctrine of beauty, which is God's gift to the world and our only true communion with Him. I am His knight, and thus have known many beauties. The arch-monastery at Drachenfels, arched and buttressed and windowed in styles rayonnant and flamboyant so that the sun, when it spills over the mountaintop, births in their pools a million more suns, each as fiery and as glad. The great battle at Nicopolis, when Lazarevic of the Serbs struck down from his own knights' hands the Sultan's banners and cried above them three times "Christ All-Mighty!" ere he turned, and charged. Aye, and our own charge thereafter, the sanguine pennon of our Order scourging the air above our heads and the fire of Iophiel staining black our lances, and our sisters (Walpurga herself among them) singing behind us while the Eldest Brethren stomped flat the janissaries.

There are other beauties I know are lost to me, as all those I set down above shall one day be lost. Such is my lot and the lot of my brethren, by God. But the sight of Walpurga and our daughter swaying, swaying, amid the candles—that beauty was, I thought, eternal. I know even as I write them that I do the scene no justice. Yet, I suspect no words exist in any tongue of earth, heaven or hell which could paint for you the picture of what I saw.

How long I watched them I say again I cannot say, only that some part of me wishes it had indeed lasted an eternity. But then the door creaked open again, and before the intruding man's first footfalls faded, the girl wriggled from Walpurga's grasp like a piglet and rushed squealing at him. She thumped into his leg with a jouster's vigor, clasped it with all four limbs, and laughed.

He stepped into the room very swiftly for a man thus encumbered, and though I only glimpsed him—brown hair cropped short, a shaven face, a scarred nose—I knew he was not me, not in this world nor any other. He first kissed the girl upon the head, and then looked at Walpurga. His eyes, I noticed, were quite blue.

Walpurga stared at him for the very briefest moment. And then she grinned a grin I once thought belonged to me and me alone, and flung her arms around his neck and kissed him *and*—

—I threw the eye from me, cursing. A moment passed as I waited for Prospero to wake and flay me, by word or look, for my foolishness. But he merely farted, snored and turned over in his slumber. I waited a moment longer. Then, like a drunkard after his flask, I chased off into the squelching dark, groping for the eye among the weeds and the bones, and above me the branches like jesters' flails rattled their mockery. Eventually I retrieved it and, sweating, bore it back to camp and there I did not sleep but instead watched yet more phantasms, a monk fastened to his scholarship.

Prospero awoke to a morning wordless as the dusk and again we witnessed no dawn but for the stars and the distant Tower, its one light an eye unlidded and aflame within the sea of Night. We walked on.

The fourth week. Across the blasted peaks, our shadows thinned unto razors by an absent sun, our heads pressed down to our breasts by the wail of winds gushed forth from some hitherto unknown mouth of hell, we met again those men who wore the Beast's pilfered face. From them, we took wounds. In payment, we beat them down. We bled them. We bit open their skulls and cracked the marrow from their ribs and dropped it sizzling in our nightfire and over it spoke the benedictions of our Order—*Break the teeth in their mouths, O God; May they be like the slug that melts away, like the stillborn child that never sees the sun*—and whetted their lives away from our swords, our axes. Blood dried in our beards. Our bones shattered and we prayed through the cloudless eves and saw again and again the fiery downfall of our Lord before that traitor His Father and we spoke His words to that dumb and unchronicled night and were reknit, the Dragon's sacrament firing our innermost humors (though it grew faint and fainter every gloamish morn). Trees uprooted themselves and made scarce at our approach. The piping of the mad and ultimate North lullabied our sleep. Down the mountains we slid into the vast gullet of the plain, the wind's fetor breathing down our necks. We stalked the dark and the stillness of deep winter stalked with us and indeed it seemed all noise (both animal and other) fled us; even the clank of our plate and the rustle of our mail muted their twin voices, as though in deference to a beast greater than themselves, and more bloodsoaked.

I made no secret now of my nightly dalliance with the giant's eye. By its light alone I passed my vigils. I slept little. I no longer prayed at lauds or vespers with Prospero. I no longer japed with him upon the trail. I no longer swaggered swords and staves with him by the light of our nightfire. Instead I longed each day for the night, that I might look upon my woman. It was her betrayals which dominated; aye indeed, soon her betrayals consumed both her lives and deaths, for (so I reasoned) was not a life lived without me—or a death in which I was no partner—not its own betrayal?

I recognized, of course, that there was a madness upon me; some strain of that flagellant's disease which seduces flesh to its own ruin, every painful moment seized upon like a new and sloppy triumph. Perhaps it lurks within us all from birth. I cannot say why that is so. Perhaps it is but one more legacy of Eden and its fall. I had not thought myself susceptible to its charm, but that is the way of the heart and the soul: they secrete within themselves their own venoms, against which they supply no antidote.

viii

Across that plain we walked until the pines again bristled the earth and we lost by degree all sense of light and thunder such that we wandered like Cain betwinned in an outer darkness, searching now for a Nod that was not. Prospero cowled his face beneath the skull of a brute, like some heathen casque from the romances. He stopped here and there along the trail, sniffing the needled earth. But what spoor he huffed up he held to himself and himself alone.

Beneath a tree vast as the very bartizan of Hell, its green limbs outstretched beneath a hunter's moon, we scratched together the makings of a flame. But now even the barest ember denied us its succor and so we slept and rose and walked again in murk, guiding ourselves hand by hand over the boles of the firs around us, themselves soft and corrugated as the flesh of babes leathered unto an age unnatural. We wandered and we wandered and the trail obscured itself from us and even the manserpents forswore our bloody friendships and I contemplated then that perhaps it was true, what men said: the dark of the world was born of woman.

But I was yet a man and mooted such thoughts to no mind but my own, for many times before had we walked into darkness, Prospero and I. We, who marched those long chill marches beneath a brazen cross; we, who turned out heathens from their hovels by dawn and warmed ourselves upon their pyres by dusk; we, who saw Scorpio and Cancer and their ill-starred ilk burn like witch's piss upon the long guttered heavens. Yet I admit, in those days Walpurga walked beside us.

Now for us the lonesome days, the drudgered nights. Now for us the memories—what few our Lord allowed us, that is.

Come one day sat we twain, chewing on those last carnal wafers we retained, savoring in them the memory of hiss and venom. Above us reigned Queen Night, with her eye the moon half shut as though she could not bear up in her heart even one glance at we, her dissolute sons. Here upon this tableau, this despondency of the earth, spoke Prospero.

"I tire of this fare."

I chewed, swallowed, chewed. "Conjure a hart, hunter, that you may practice your venery and save our aching jaws."

Prospero stared out across that rock on which we sat and the light of the flame did not touch him nor did the glower of the moon kiss him and his hair like a sailor's weeds salt-tangled by the sea hung down into his face. The wind shifted and I stood and scratched my beard.

"Bacon, better yet. Beard us a boar, that I might smoke his crackling upon an open flame."

Prospero looked at me sidelong now, and grinned. "We've some bacon still. Long rashers of it."

I frowned down at him. I crossed myself, and he laughed.

"Long the rashers of the bacon; yet longer still the face of fell Hieronymus." He reached with his hand into that aborted ember we misnamed our fire and rooted among its coals as though there existed one right and proper for his purpose, some biscuit of hell he might swipe fresh from its hearth. When he found him just one such cinder, he plucked it smoking from its ashes and rolled it this way then that in his hand, and it lit his face from below like the lakes of Hell light their inmate angels, scattered fallen by the Father's judgment. Then he flicked it at me.

"God's wounds and blind you," I said, swiping at my beard where cooked now that errant flame. "Blackheart! Blackguard!"

Prospero laughed and laughed again. "Bacon, quoth the knight. Well smoke yourself, sir Pallamedes! Sooty bearded you were, and sooty bearded you shall remain."

At last, after much undignified swattings and pattings, I quenched the coal and, smoke curling now from the curls of my beard, I couched my gaze at Prospero's mirth-scarred face. "Why this buffoonery?"

He passed a hand over his face, and when again his fingers unshielded him, his mouth lay straight and unsmiling as any lance. "How else," he said, "should a man lighten his brother up?"

My cheeks reddened and I stood, fingering at my side the giant's eye and I admit, I stalked off in what a mind less generous might generously term a huff. Yet I walked not one stride distant ere Prospero clapped hands upon my spaulder. "My apologies, brother. An ill-timed jape."

I snorted breath through my nose. My fists clenched and unclenched. Had I hooves, no doubt they would have pawed furrows through the stone. "Unhand me."

He did not. Such is the pride of brothers. "Speak, man, if speak you must. Grievances oft wilt beneath the fresh air, quoth the tanner to his wife."

But I said nothing. Instead I shrugged my shoulders, dipped my hips and thereby shucked off his grip. Grinning, Prospero struck a stance and reached for my wrist. I shoved him and he snatched for my spaulder, missed, then settled for my couter. Laughing now despite myself, I snaked my arm down then up, noosing it over his head. But he wrenched back, and when he could not loosen my grip, slammed his greave into my knee. I gritted my teeth against the dagger of that pain, feinted a drop, slapped down his hands, then clenched my own again behind his neck. He dug a fist into my throat, choking a curse from me.

"What game is this, Mordred?" I said, but he offered me no chuckling riposte, only the deep growl of a beast frothed unto madness. I loosened my grip and attempted a step back but he bulled into me, clawing now like a savage for his hold. I cursed again, hooked my arms over his pauldron, his couter, and twisted as he rushed. We clanked into a tree and I'd him half-thrown over my hip ere I saw the vacant look glazing his eyes, the black fog staining his breath. I unclasped him and stepped away as though scalded. He hunched against the tree, his breastplate heaving as though he drowned in his own choler. His breath smoked the air.

"Hell hath no limits, nor is circumscribed," he said, "in one self place, but where we are is hell. And where hell is, there must we ever be." In his voice echoed all ebon-painted Dis's choir. His teeth glowed red.

"Brother," I said, crossing myself, "remember yourself. You are not He."

He looked at me and tears crimsoned his eyes. "Pater," he said, and "proditor" and then a long string of words slurred free of him in that language which prefigured Babel's siege and from his tongue more smoke wafted and I drew my sword. Yet even as I took my guard, I lamented that no nun stood by our sides, quill in hand, ready to record his visions of the primordial War and so add (by even one strophe more) to that everlasting evershifting chronicle of our Lord's Fall. But I did not lament long, for almost at once Prospero ceased his babbling and stepped forward and I pointed my blade at him. He stepped again, and I sang aloud that last song of our Order, which few but we brothers ever may hear. Prospero stepped a third time and I breathed out and eyed the white line of his throat above his tattered mail and then willed myself to look him in the eye. Such is the love of brothers.

But then Prospero lunged and stars burst before my eyes and my ears rang and before I realized he'd thrown me, his hands raked my throat. I punched the side of his head with the pommel of my sword, but there was no strength in the blow. My vision narrowed and I smelt again the horrid, sweet perfume of his breath and he muttered in my ear in a tongue not his own. I worked my legs under me, hoping to buck him to one side but he gripped my wrist and said to me in antique Saxon, "Michael, O brother, where cleavest thy brand?"

I wrenched my hand and it did not move, for such is the might of the afflicted. I butted him in the mouth with my head and quick as a cat he clouted me across the chin and all strength fled me. My gorge boiled up into my throat and the world whirled like a dervish of the Saracens, though I did not move, and I knew then I might die. But perhaps some saint smiled upon me, for even as I so thought, Prospero blinked and stumbled and rolled from me, and when he again upturned his face towards me, it was clean and unmaddened.

"I am," he gasped. His lips worked, silent as a fish who, hooked free of its pelagic keep, gulps now the unwholesome venomed air. Slowly, his mouth closed and his eyes regained that luster which some call the Soul and which the wise call the Gnosis and which, no matter the name one carves upon it, forever badges Man above those dumb beasts who were once (and shall one day be again) his kin. I sheathed my sword and Prospero's face twisted, as though shamed by his redeemed faculties.

"How long?" Prospero said.

"Longer than your doxy tells you she needs," I rasped, "but shorter than the truth."

Prospero did not laugh. He pawed his face, as though some other man's flesh might clad his bones and make them foreign.

"What did I say?" he said, but before I could answer he waved his hand. "No. It is nothing."

"It is our blessing, the Catechism says, to speak Christ's—" I said, before he looked at me. I coughed. "My apologies, brother."

"The fault is not yours. It is nothing, I said." He shuffled his feet. "Did I strike you?"

A knight does not lie to his brother, so I said naught. Prospero sighed.

"It grows more frequent, this madness," said he. "I thought perhaps this hunt—" his voice trailed off and he shook his head. I said nothing. At length, he thumbed his mustache and looked away from me, towards the face of night. Moments passed, unbroken in their solitude but for the wind.

"I am vexed," he said at last. "Most sorely vexed."

I leaned back against the flat rock on which we'd sat, and rubbed my throat. "Such is the feast of Man, I daresay. Vexation his bread and vitriol his wine and death his just dessert."

"Is that all we are? Feasters and then corpses?"

"What more might a man be," I said, and regretted it in the instant, for it was unworthy. Yet words, like arrows, cannot be unloosed.

Prospero, perhaps catching full in his heart my fletched voice, scowled. "Much more, I should imagine a man. A thinker, and a builder, and a doer of great deeds."

"A slayer."

Prospero grunted. "A hunter, belike."

I laughed a hangman's laugh, cold and rough as hempen knots. "So you would say, I suppose. For my part, name me slayer, name me reaver, name me *knight* ere you anoint me something so foolish as a hunter."

"You wrong yourself, then, as is your wont these days. You divorce yourself from the quintessence. That is unvirtuous."

My knuckles voiced, by their crackle, my discontent. "Pray tell."

Prospero saluted me with two fingers. "As you will. Consider the Hunt. The entire race of Man stems in its every branch and flower from that plain and verdant root we name the Huntsman, who stalked (and in some nighted corners stalks yet) those forests which once crowned our Earth in her virgin youth. And consider likewise that it is as the Athenian said: all that which comes after partakes (in its essence) something of that which came before. Therefore, if all Men stem from the Hunter, the Hunt (which so ordered the Hunter's life) must remain locked within that heart all Men share."

I clapped as men clap when their rival breaks a lance, yet keeps his seat. "Well spoken."

He mocked a bow. "Phial for me your tears, that I might nourish myself on them later." He sniffed. "They shall taste of salt and smoke, I wager. Much like the Salaca, whose mouth we now approach."

That set my heart a-thumping. "Say again?"

"The Salaca, brother," he said, his voice slurring somewhat at the edge. "We near it now. Our hunt concludes. A low hunt, of sows and sucklings, I daresay. One yearns for the boar, betimes."

I looked away from his eyes—knowing there what resident flame I would behold—and towards his hands. They curled, pale-knuckled, around his axe. The sight cheered me little. I shall waste no time on our mutual affliction, nor its stigmata—you who read this account shall already know more of it than I can tell. Less among you may know, however, that to speak of said affliction to the afflicted themselves, in the nascence of their frenzy, never calms them. Rather, like oil upon flame, it only calls forth our Lord's hallowed rage all the swifter, and all the stronger. Walpurga taught me this—and by certain scars, verified her testimony (and my shame).

Bearing that in mind, I spoke (as Walpurga once spoke to me) as though he were himself unridden by the God.

"Perhaps you speak truly, brother. We are all huntsmen. Nor is the hunt of beasts the only one worth pursuing. After all, who among our estate has not known the love of a woman, and the joy by which it is attained when, by arduous action, it is hunted? And who does not know the contempt with which said love is condemned when, by lazy gold, we purchase its delight?"

I thought perhaps this would cheer him—for Prospero lived on debate as other men might live by bread and wine. And indeed, other times, in other places, just such a gambit had succeeded. But here, Prospero's face, hitherto animated by his more melancholic humors, now slackened, assuming in its posture the brute rapture of a martyr nailed, by cold iron, to his pyre.

"As one great furnace flamed," he said, "yet from those flames no light, but rather darkness visible served only to discover sights of woe, regions of sorrow, doleful shades, where peace and rest can never dwell, hope never comes that comes to all; but torture without end still urges, and a fiery deluge, fed with ever-burning sulfur unconsumed: this the Eternal Tyrant hath prepared."

Stepping back, I thrust my sword forward into that guard we call the Iron Gate and prayed Prospero would (in his madness) strike, if again he struck, slower than last he had.

But he smote naught. He stood swaying, his axe hung loose in his grip, his eyes again the eyes of a beast, black and old and unhallowed. He mumbled something. Against my better judgment, I edged a half-step nearer.

"Speak louder, brother. And remember who you are."

He coughed, and looked at me like a man bewildered. "A knight endures, I said. Yet, no knight endures forever." He shook his head. "Did I not?"

No water, not even the spume of Paradise, ever cooled a man deeper, or more swiftly. "You did," I said, "indeed you did." Smiling as man must at a doom averted, I sheathed my sword. Prospero squinted at me, his gaze combing my own as if he might louse from me my falsehoods. But then he shrugged and clapped my shoulder and sat down beside me upon our pine-sheltered rock. So squatted we there, nooked in mutual silence as Queen Night perished, her feet burned away already by her jealous lover the Sun, and the clouds (like that smoke which ferries the warlock's soul to Hell) rose and danced and tickled with their fumes the very nose of their lady the Night, as if in her death she might yet deserve some pleasure.

It was the first true dawn we'd seen in some time. Perhaps that is why we did not hear them approach us until they stood nigh upon our greaves. I turned just as the first one, sword in hand, yanked from his crown the red shroud of his capirote. Dawn glanced from his slitted eyes. When he hissed, venom dripped sizzling from his fangs.

ix

The manserpent hewed at me, and I parried. Slumber-slow, my hands, and nightmare-weak, and the manserpent's blade—some curved monstrosity forged from the dreams of a mad Turk—crushed my scabbarded blade aside and clanged hard into my rerebrace. Black pain seared me and I grunted and fell, blood squirting from my arm.

The manserpent hissed and hewed again but I rolled aside, more from luck than any skill, and its blade bit deep into the earth. Before it could resume its guard, I charged it, blade clasped low in the guard of the half-sword. I stuck it through the gut but it clouted me about the face and bore me down all the same. We tumbled and I lost my sword and the manserpent drew from its belt a dirk and bared its fangs at me and they dripped pregnant with their venom and when I grabbed for its neck to stay their bite, it stabbed me under the arm.

Perhaps it says much of me that at first I thought not of the pain (which was considerable) but of my death and its shame: slain not even by that Beast which we hunted but by its bastard byblow. A voice within me—you shall know the one, I think, for in every man's ear it must sometimes whisper—said this was no more and no less a death than that which I deserved. The manserpent leaned over me and I swear some mirth glinted in its eyes, as though it likewise heard this voice and shared its estimation of my character, of my doom.

I spat blood in its face. It snapped its fangs and hissed again and again and again and now it screamed and that's when at last I saw the pike of Prospero's axe peck through its neck. He yanked the creature up like a man gigging a fish and with its last breath it stabbed him too, nailing his hand to his axe-haft. He cursed and the axe drooped and the manserpent slid from it and I picked up my sword and crawled to the thing and thrust it through the eye. It whimpered like a page dead upon his father's field, and tried to speak to me in a man's voice (as so often they did) and its face was (despite its fangs) like any other son of Adam. But then I twisted the blade—for I am that sort of man—and it writhed and shat and was dead.

I rolled to my back and breathed hard. Prospero plucked the dirk from his hand, and blood pinked its blade. He frowned at it, then licked it clean and tossed it over his shoulder.

Stooping, he pulled me to my feet and unclasped from his belt that hinged and silvered skull which all knights of our Order bear. From it, he drew forth a flask fashioned in the shape of a woman's body, its aspect naked and abundant (and resplendent in said abundance) as the Virgin ripened ere our Savior's birth. Within this flask smoldered our last stock of the thrice-consecrated Blood, of the holy, ash-dry Flesh. Without Walpurga or some other sister of the Order, no more would be forthcoming; yet without imbibing it, the hallowed fire of the saints would not be ours to wield.

Prospero assayed our wounds with a glance. Wordlessly, he pushed towards me the Blood and the Flesh. His eyes held within them no rebuke.

The flask rattled when I passed it back to Prospero. He sipped, then bandaged up his hand. He said something I did not hear, and laughed.

That night, after we'd marched a new path across the forested plain, we banked high our renewed fire and discussed the hunt. Excitement ruled Prospero; the manserpents' breads, poached upon our flame, had captained him towards a fresh trail of the Beast's spoor, and the Tower, visible once more upon the dim horizon, no longer fled our approach. He spent long moments pontificating on the vagaries of tracks and wind direction and the whispered advice of angels. Yet, pondering already my next vision of Walpurga, fondling anew the giant's eye upon my belt, I heard little. It was only once Prospero's speech turned towards our remaining stock of the Sacrament that I took true notice.

"—enough only for one more imbibing," he said, and I raised my head.

"We arsenal it away for our escape," I said at once. "We know not what travails we might need conquer ere we spring ourselves from this gaol."

Prospero smiled at me. Often he smiled these days and nights, and laughed. A strange thing too, for though always had I known him as a smiling, laughing man, it was only now—in this weird, wave-besotted place—that I realized how little he'd smiled this past year, how rare he'd wielded the belly-wrought bludgeon of his laugh.

"A rare jest, Hieronymus," he said. "Surely, we hoard it all for our final encounter with the Beast."

"If that be our final hurdle, let it be so. Elsewise, I scarce hold to it. A folly, this mad pursuit."

Prospero combed a hand through the tangle of his beard and sat back against a rock. "A folly, is it? A quest, I call it."

"Six of one, said the banker, or a half dozen of the other."

Prospero laughed. "Do not lie, brother. Never have you met a banker."

"Even so. A folly, I say."

"We seek a great foe. What could be less a folly?"

"The last words, I reckon, of many a great fool."

"Perhaps." Prospero leaned his head back, and did not speak for a moment. When at last he did, there was a shadow to his smile. "The Knight of Foxes. Was his pursuit a folly?"

"It led us here," I said after a moment's contemplation. "But no. He despoiled our lands. He thieved from our ships. His death was warranted."

"*Warranted*," Prospero said, and spat. "Are we legists, to speak of warrants and whyfores? Tell it true: he was a no-account pirate who pillaged grain and cloth from peasants."

"He was a knight."

"He was a cretin. The latest in a long line of witch-killings, bandit hunts, and inquisitions. Is that our vocation, you think? Cleaving down men deemed heretic by some fat bishop on his couch?"

"As the wise man said: *caedite eos.*"

"*Novit enim Dominus qui sunt eius*," Prospero said, the words rattled off as though invested in him by a mind rote and other than his own.

"A wisdom," I said.

Prospero scowled. "I darenot gainsay it. Yet is it the prowess of old Arthur and his table round? Is it worthy of that Christ, hurled headlong flaming from his heavened throne, whose cause we bear?" He looked away and his gaze augured the night, as though he might dig forth from its shadow some answer to a question unasked. "Your initiation to the Order. It was bloody?"

My nose wrinkled. My cheeks burned. "I do not recall it," I said, which was—in the broadest sense—true.

Prospero was not gulled. "Nor do I recall my own. Yet the body remembers, does it not? And the soul too, if only in our dreams." He frowned. "How much of your life before the Order can you recall?" He did not await my response but forged onward. "My mind bears snippets, mere snippets. Less every day, as well you know. My mother and grandmother in our keep, smiling. My brother, I think, or perhaps an uncle, training in the tiltyard." He frowned deeper. "The reek of fire. The scent of blood."

I said nothing for a time. The flame spat and crackled, and I shook my head. "We sacrifice much. We gain more."

"Do we?" Prospero said.

"Of course."

Prospero shook his head. "I am not so certain. What do you recall of your father?"

I sighed. Chasing after such memories was like capturing swallows unlimed by the falcon's claw—they flittered close then far, consenting only to a glimpse, a touch, a smell, but never allowing themselves to be grasped in full. Yet for Prospero's sake, I attempted.

"He was a good man. He had blue eyes, and a long beard. He loved me. He loved my mother."

"Your mother, you say. Was she not his wife?"

"I do not recall."

Prospero did not smile, but I knew by the glint of his eye he thought that admission a blow landed. "Aye, just so. When you made your initiation to our order, did you imagine this was all it would be? Hunting the Knight of Foxes and his ilk? Burning peasants and rooting out heretics? Awaiting every day the time when we shall lose ourselves entirely to the Sacrament and thereafter must (if we not perish in our ignominy) submit to the *reconciliatio extremum* and take our place entombed among the Eldest Brethren, sleeping the sleep of death in our silvern cages until the hour comes and we hear the song of our sisters once more? Is that why we wield the Black Flame of Iophiel? Is that why we bib down the Blood and the Flesh? Your father was a good man, you say. Would he look upon you now, and see the same?"

"He would see a knight."

Prospero eyed me. "For want of rope, Man shall noose himself with his own tongue, quoth the scholar."

"If I am noosed, then let it be by my own hand and none other. Such is the freedom of a knight."

"Is it? Our teachers and troubadours stuffed our minds with the tales of our fathers—Aristotle and Arthur; Christ and Chretien. Our swordmasters swelled our thews with the steps and strikes of our fathers' fathers. Our thoughts tread again the paths cut first by our forebears' minds. Thus we hop and hew in the image of our fathers, and the fathers of our fathers. How might we then count ourselves new men, and not but shades of elder days, fleshed afresh in gaudy youth? Do we martyr ourselves upon knighthood's altar of our own volition, or does some greater mind print its thumb upon us and so mold us into familiar shape? What will lies therein? What choice? Are we men, or the echoes of men, seeded once and springing forever from the same tired earth, watered forevermore by chivalry's iron unguent?"

"The son is not the father, nor the father of the father. A knight carves his own destiny. This we do in image of the Christ."

"Aye, perhaps. But if so, then should we not be more than our fathers, as He is more than His? How far might the world fall, if we do not better the works of those before us? Should we not conquer where they faltered?"

"Do we not?"

Prospero frowned, and did not answer.

"Long have we labored beneath the Dragon's banner," I said. "I would not have thought it a discomfort to you."

Prospero stared into the fire. "*Comfort.*" He made the word a slur. "That is the whole of the problem. No knight should ever be so. Comfort kills the knight, and births in his place the coward. What comfort knew Lancelot? What comfort knew Arthur? Nay, I spit on comfort. It is the wine of sybarites and the bread of villeins."

We sat in silence then, our gazes staked each to the nightfire's blaze. In its furnace, a man may see all things, both in their ending and their beginning, and at last—motivated, perhaps, by those unbodied prophecies—I spoke.

"Prospero," I said. "Why this melancholy? Why this mad hunt?"

He looked at me, and ran his hand through his beard and was inscrutable amid his masking shadows. "The Sacrament of our Order has thieved much from me. I no longer recall my father's name. I no longer recall my mother's voice, or my sister's, or my brother's. They are lost to me. But this, I recall.

"I was young—a sprat, knee-high and knot-limbed. In the hills surrounding my father's keep, a wolf slew sheep. This was no common wolf. It feared neither blade nor bow nor flame. It ate children, and killed their fathers when they hunted it down. In this, I say, it differed little from my father. A hard man, he was. He ruled with an iron fist, and his people loved him little. Perhaps that is why the women soon whispered this wolf was in truth a knight, cursed by some heathenry blown down from the utter north to take the shape of a beast and feast upon the flesh of man. I know not who said it first, but soon all the countryfolk bleated that tale. Perhaps it was even true, I cannot say. I have seen the berserks of the Svears and the wolfskins of the Balts, and truly it is as the philosopher said: *homo homini lupus est.* Anyways. They came to my father, all those headmen in their peasant finery, and demanded he slay the beast. 'What man may slay a monster,' they said, 'but another monster?'

"I thought my father would slay them on the spot for their impertinence. He was that sort of man. But this time, at least, he did not cut them down. Instead, he sat upon his throne and listened. Eventually the peasants departed and still, my father stared into the flame of our hearth. He took thence to the chapel, where he prayed amid the candles and the night. Come morning, he broke his vigil. What he saw within the flames or the chapel, no man now may say, but he left the altar and armed himself. He took up his lance, his sword, and his steed. He rode out into the hills, alone. I watched from the keep. Forest jacketed the hills, so deep and so dark a man could not see the sun once he entered. Before my father entered that forest, he rode three times round the castle. He held his lance in the air, and the sun glanced from it like fire. 'Death!' he cried. 'Death! Death!'"

Silence thereafter.

"Did he slay the wolf," I said.

Prospero smiled. "I do not recall."

I laughed, and yet felt myself in some sense chastened. We sat again for a time, and I looked from our fire into the wavelicked sky and in it I beheld an umber stained black by some sin ancestral of all other oiled perfidy, such that by standing in it one felt likewise slicked.

Prospero thudded a hand onto my shoulder, and I startled.

"Your woman's loss pains you."

"She is not lost."

"Do your memories of her dim?"

I looked at him. "Never."

Prospero held up his hands. "As you say, as you say."

"She is not lost."

"Aye." He paused, then grinned, as though to pillow a blow. "If she were though, perhaps you would bleed the less, and slay the more."

"Perhaps."

"You mourn, brother."

I looked at him, then back to the flame. "Not I."

"You droop."

"I hang, conceivably. One fingersbreadth from the ground, by some measure."

"Aye, or from the nearest tree, I fear, every morning ere I see you mooning into yonder giant's loosened light."

I shrugged. "When it rains, I get no less wet than other men. Yet no more, either. When Lancelot thought Guinevere burnt to her bane, he wept. I am not so moist a man as he, yet nor am I stone. What of it?"

Prospero slapped my back. "Ah, your lady's gotten bane is what you fear? Her piercing by lance, by sword, by any other prick of pike that might fill a woman to her death, however little?"

"It crosses the mind."

"Then let it cross and leave and stay gone." Prospero waved his hand, as if assessing and dismissing the perfidy of all womankind. "A wench is like a coin—a man borrows her for the moment. He shall spend her, or she shall spend herself."

"Walpurga is no coin."

Prospero considered this. "Perhaps not." He looked me over. "Yet it is as the prophet foretold: 'one woe is past; and, behold, there come two woes more hereafter.'"

I peered around us, as though I might rustle from the shade some spare sorrows, cast-off by their better days. "Indeed? I see no more women hereabouts. Nor any more Italians."

Prospero laughed, but not for long. "You bear wounds, brother. Wounds you would not have taken in days gone."

"Aye, well."

"Well, aye. You fell today when yesteryear you would not have. I note you offer no reason for it. Well, I am not so meek. You divide yourself, and are weakened. Heed the lessons of the elder knights. What doomed Lancelot, but for a woman's love? What doomed Arthur? Aye, and Tristan too! They lied to themselves, thinking the sweetness of the lie a tonic to its scourge. You pursue the same folly, I wager."

Whatever good humor I'd maintained leaked from me as pus from a boil. "Keep private your further counsels on this matter, sir. I shall return to Walpurga. Such is my vow."

Prospero smiled. "As you say. You are loyal to her. It is a virtue. But mark me: what you seek in her is not love. Like Erec with his Enide, you seek the bed over the sword. Like him, you dilute yourself in her. Aye, and who would not? The heart whispers of comfort to the mind, and its tongue is a flap of gold."

And here Prospero leaned in close, like a man imparting the utmost key of creation. "The heart, I tell you, *lies*. It would cozen a man from all the red raw *life* of the world! It would pillow away all the sweating truths of body and soul. It would comfort a man to blackest damnation, if it could. Why, I cannot say. The Father's last whisper, echoing down from the Garden, perhaps. Our hearts would slave us to comfort. Yet, we are no slaves."

I stood. "You've argued your piece, Aristotle. Let your rhetoric work, if work it shall. In the meantime, sleep. I've the first watch."

Prospero sat unyielding, locked as some man into a covenant, a terrible covenant, himself anointed to himself. Perhaps that is the relationship of all men to their soul—every man piloted toward his own doom by a hand he himself owns, but does not wield.

Then he waved his hand as if offering a benediction and said, "aye, aye." He took his station on the farside of the fire, his axe clutched tight to him as a lover, and slept.

I kept watch. My hands prodded at my own wounds, as though the pain therefrom might awaken in me some fit answer to his words. The giant's eye weighed heavy upon my hip.

𝔗he night passed slow.

Prospero's words worked on me like a lindwurm's bile, boiling me up with a fever once foreign to my flesh. Again and again, I thought on it: my strength, sapped by a woman's heart. A ludicrous notion, to my mind. And yet, the scars upon my body—fading already, by the grace of God and the Dragon—bore witness, perhaps, to a different tale.

I thought too of comfort, and the long days abed I'd spent with Walpurga, the music of her laughter and the brush of her kisses painting for me a Paradise unparalleled since the Fall.

Finally, I thought of our work with the Order ere our exile into this wavescummed gaol: the burnings, the inquisitions, the raids. Though I admitted no word of it to Prospero—or to any man living—I too dreamed of them betimes, and thought myself alone in my affliction. I dreamed of Saletsa, of the Salaca long, low and cold, of the pines refulgent in their dark and the men and the women and the children walking in file across the snow toward the maw of night. Behind them, fire and the songs of monks and the slapping of the whips of righteous men, and their own footprints, red upon the snow.

And yet what man may trust a dream? Prospero was not wrong; the Sacrament thieves much from us. I recalled those dreams more brightly than the day itself and so perhaps the day was no less and no more than the dream itself, and thus I was no more and no less a sinner than I was a dreamer. Aye and is that not a blessed state to which so many men—in their wineskins and in their women and in the long dilute drain of their lives—is that not a state to which they much aspire? Yet the common man is mud and his dreams are mud—and so were I to be that to which he aspires, was I then any less a clod of unreckoned dirt? What a man might you birth for lack of a memory—what an orphan, what a bastard?

Cloud-robed Night descended—no moon again, its absence a hollow blade within the scabbard of the sky—and instead beheld I its imitator the Tower with his strobing glare, his ochred ray in which far-off bats whirled and dipped with wings like dragons made miniature by the widening of the world. I thought then that it was true, what Walpurga told me when last my chest cushioned her head: night hallows the world. It cleaves from it the shameless shades of day and leaves in their place the beating heart of the earth. All things at night reveal themselves in light and shadow, in black and white, and so they reveal a truth of the world, which is that all we dwellers in it and of it are ourselves carven from the light and the dark and in us no other paints may muddy that hue. We are children of the bright moon and the black sky, and all the spaces betwixt, and the lonesome dark we see beyond is only our own soul's thread unspooled. Prospero spoke no lies: in the silvered nights of yore, our forefathers hunted the great creatures of the weald and slew them and gnashed them down to their marrowbones and made of themselves the sovereign beasts of the earth, crowned in gore. We are still the children of those fathers, of those beasts.

I thought then of my own father, and his father, and what few memories of them I retained, misered away like gold within a wyrmling's hoard. I thought, at last, of Prospero's tale of his father and the wolf. *What man may slay a monster, they said, but another monster?*

I frowned. Then, I stood and walked from our fire into the woods. I cut two staves from a nearby tree while Prospero slept and commenced whittling them each to a longsword's stature.

Pale dawn routed from the sky night's black legions, and I prodded Prospero awake. He woke as the cat does, all at once. He glanced at the staves, then at me. "Witches?"

"Switches, conceivably." I tossed him one and he plucked it from the air. "On your guard, brother. If I am to bleed less in battle I must sweat more in the list, I daresay."

Prospero grinned and laughed and, standing, sketched a salute with his staff. "Have at it then."

We fenced with our staves through the hour of lauds and into prime, then hunted on in pursuit of the Beast.

The next weeks passed in a fugue, each day blurring into its brothers. By day, we rose and prayed and tracked the Beast. By night, we fenced and wrestled by firelight in full armor, in half armor, in our tattered pourpoints and all combinations thereof. I did not look upon the giant's eye. Yet nor did I cast it into ruin. This too was its own prayer, of a kind.

We shivered amid the cold; we sweltered in the heat. Bruises painted us from nose to knee, blooming in purples and blacks and faded, aureate bursts. We tasted our own blood and our own sweat and the dust of the world, and all were themselves transmuted to a wine of sorts, a communion with the ironmost edge of the earth.

xi

We trekked across a land made one vast fortress by the hands of collosi undreamt by any man born downstream of Eden's fall. Spires of black stone hung gibbeted from the seaswept sky, their corpses barren of all life but that of rats and crows and all those other skinscraping scavengers of the world. Animate bones, eyes alight with the flames of hell, bore down at us by the dwindling stars. They whispered words in dead languages; their fingers, bare of all harnessing flesh, thrust for our eyes, for our mouths, for the warm and pulsing throats buried deep within the thickets of our beards. We soothed them to their slumber with the hammer of Prospero's axe, with the pommel of my longsword, with our gauntlets, our poleyns, with the very hoarse of our tongues, which spoke to them the long and winding catechism of our Order as the sun knelt down amid the bleeding west and the moon rose triplet in the north and impaled our shadows to our corselets like black banners waving, waving in the wind.

The Tower rose steaming from the morning mist and Prospero saw it and cried out and thumped my back and I cheered alongside him. The spoor of the Beast thickened and we heard by dawn and dusk the long crow of its call, like unto some basilisk fathered in ancient days from an egg not its own.

Amid the ruins of a keep of brick, the slitted eyes of its windows shrouded by tapestries woven in the rotting purples and scabbish reds of a kingdom long-dead, we plotted our final essay. We were ourselves but one hue shy of the grave: our cheeks sunken, our eyes sepulchred within their sockets, our limbs racked tight to their frames, our ebon plate strung up and over with the pelts and bones of our many victims. As we made our ultimate conclave, I reckon we looked like nothing so much as the prince-knights of all ghouldom, winkled forth from our dens to gnaw one last marrow from the bones of the world.

I spoke first. "We shall approach it as one does a man in the melee: we corner it. One of us holds its regard. The other lances it." We made other arrangements, which I shall not belabor. To them all, Prospero nodded his agreement.

A simple plan for simple men. The man who drew the Beast's attention drew the harsher duty. Naturally, we both clamored for it. We debated the finer points of our argument in knightly fashion: which is to say, we fought for it. Prospero bested me three falls to two, and so won the honor. I begrudged him but a little.

We prepared ourselves thereafter. I sat upon a tumbled statue, its face divorced from its greater whole, leaving in its place a blank expanse like some changeling foisted upon the world from a place other than itself. I whetted my longsword, oiled it and was content. Prospero stood near, tinking dents from his harness with a hammer unsuited to the task. Moments passed and he tired of his futilities and rose and paced and muttered, an old wolf gaunt and grizzled and red about the muzzle. I wondered then if he was not himself, if the memories like shadows cast upon the cavern of his mind by the fiery sacrament of our Lord had not now consumed him, and this creature which wore his face was not the man but his successor, a blade whetted down to its final burning edge, a sword unslaked and unslakeable.

Yet if any such maudlin scratchings afflicted the man himself, he brooked no outward sign. He smiled and sang beneath his breath a tuneless song of death, such as men sing after battle whilst scalping heathen heads.

"We shall conquer," he said as we finished strapping ourselves into the remnants of our plate. Joy beamed from him, and I did not gainsay him, for I too felt its inkling. Aye, and more than an inkling mayhaps.

I rasped from my sword the last of its rust. Then without ceremony I unlidded the Sacrament from its housing skull. Prospero, head bowed in prayer, looked up. He shook his head.

"Belay yon uncorking. We know not what lies beyond the Beast. We may need it for our escape." He winked at me. "Or would you not return now to your Walpurga?"

I looked at him, thinking he japed. Seeing he was serious, I frowned. "You are a strange man, Prospero. Were you brother to Cain himself you would keep him close, for all the murder in his eyes, I darenot doubt it."

Prospero laughed. "Nay, not so strange! I do not subscribe to Cain's folly: I *am* my brother's keeper." He punched my shoulder. "If he bleeds, let me patch him up."

xii

We picked our way over the skull of a shattered donjon, its windows excavated like the tombs of heathen kings, all their bones picked clean of gold and laid bare to the breath of a lesser world. We saw no moon nor star nor sun nor even the foam-tongued waves who occulted them all beneath their lip and cheek. Now only the void ceilinged us, as though we ourselves delved into some tomb, diggers of our own grave, fooled by notions and knowings beyond our ken. In the distance, keeps like mountains fanged the horizon and all of that august range were dark but one which burned with a light its own and it was a corpselight, wan and green and fell. By that torch alone, Prospero reckoned our course.

Rubble and ruin thickened our way. We stepped. We hobbled. In some places we crawled, beasts cast down by a hand higher than our own, prophets of a future man, four-limbed and lost. But never did we halt.

Across our path loomed a statue of a king, his eyes marbled and forlorn and cracked beneath our tread, and us with no notion of his majesty other than that which bare stone may say. Left and right of us crumbled altars to gods forgotten and gods known and gods not-yet-known but for the long march of years ere their debut in blood and thunder. Our strides shortened. Our grips tightened over our swords, our axes.

Nearer crept the Tower, its light now an elder sun cold within its ancient bed the sky. Sparks from its flame wandered like stars across the aether, and I wondered if perhaps we did not near the end of all things, or else their beginning.

The ruins steepled into a mound. We walked, then clambered, then clawed our way to its summit where bronze and iron latticed themselves into a frame depicting forms ichthyic and chiropteran. From that vantage the wind blew down upon us and for a moment I thought I heard within its moans and its beatings those jigging rhythms of the playful dead who pipe and drum their dance upon gray Acheron's shore. I looked left then right, as though I might hunt down these importunate pipers by eye alone, until Prospero clapped a hand to my bascinet and I turned and beheld the Beast.

It nested down before a bridge of swords, its bedding the dusted bones of heroes past, its pillow their grinning skulls. The bridge itself was a tangled thing, as though all the blades of Hell's hosts lay thrust upon and in and through one another in one general and pandaemoniac orgy. Gore crusted their edges; the heads of men jewelled their hilts, their pommels. Dust carpeted its further span, a space untrod (or so it seemed) by mortal feet for years unreckoned.

Prospero and I conferred then separated, each picking our own way through the ruins towards the Beast. I was to lie in wait while Prospero provoked it. Once done, I would spring upon it and wreak its death.

But the ruins over which we stalked possessed humors of their own it seemed, for within moments of our parting I lost sight of Prospero and it was as though a mouth of stone nethered him into some other oubliette, distant of God and man alike. Yet the Beast remained in view, fixed firm as the Morningstar himself within Judecca's lake. I found my vantage and there awaited Prospero's emergence.

Idle hands are the devil's plaything, they say. Perhaps that is so, for as I waited—I know not how long, for the sun and moon and stars still hung obscured within that sea we termed the sky—my hands crept towards my belt and unhooked from its tether the giant's eye.

In the thoughtless manner of the drinker with his flagon—of the lover with his maiden's hand—I brought the eye before my face, *and*—

—*Walpurga* knelt before a fire. New scars ornamented her face. Corpses in the armor of knights stood congressed about her, and beneath their heaumes' dented brows, pale eyes blazed.

Walpurga herself wore a gown of deepest, night-born purple and a coronet of brightest, day-kissed silver, and in these two garments I thought one might read all there was to know of her, for it seemed to me she was in her every manner compounded of two things and two things only and these were the fair dusk and the dour dawn, which in her eyes alone mixed their humors and concocted from themselves some twilight unconquered by the hands of Man.

She stared into the flame—into my own eyes, it seemed—and her eyes widened as if in recognition. She reached out with her hand— the one of bone, not the one of flesh—into the flame, and her lips parted and spoke and I could not hear, *I could not hear* and her hand reached out and ou*t and*—

—*Prospero's* cry rent the air: rage and pain welded each to the other, loud and gurgling at first but then—sudden as a noose's drop— ended.

I looked and saw him, clutched by the chest within the Beast's mouth, its fangs sunk to their roots in him, and I roared and cast down the giant's eye upon the earth and smote it with my sword and it shattered like the dreams of Eve within the Garden and then I was moving, my sword held high and the death-prayer of my Order burning like a tongue of flame upon my blistered lips.

I reached the Beast and Prospero hung limp in its jaws like a corn doll in a wolfdog's grip, and indeed like a dog it shook him. I lunged a thrust at its eye and its black blood spurted and it flung Prospero aside and snapped at me and I cut it again and again and it bled and drew back. We stalked each other then, circling as fencers on the field of honor. I feinted a step and a thrust and the Beast hopped back, strange and dainty on its stag-hoofed heels. Then its head darted forward and the first I knew of it was the grate of my own bones against its fangs. I looked down at the teeth piercing my side. I fell.

The Beast loomed over me. Its mane—for I saw now it had a mane, stiff and full like the lions of far Afric—dipped itself in my blood. Its breath huffed in my ear. Then it stood tall, its square-tipped snout flung high, and I saw in it my death if I did not rise.

I say this now, for it must be said: few tasks demand more of a man than rising after he has been struck down. Your gorge billows up into your throat; your breath betrays you, razing your lungs to flake and ash; aye indeed, your very mind turns perjure, clasping hand in hand with those dread twins, Death and Surrender, and whispering their mingled perfidies into your ear: *rise not. It shall end soon. Rise not. Sleep, dreamer, sleep. Rise not.*

If ever you have labored at a weight and felt your arms tremble beneath its burden and known you must drop it or else unpeel yourself at the joints, then you have some notion of the task. To let go, to let the weight drop, it is the softest breathiest balm, like the breeze upon the blacksmith's face as he turns sweating from his forge. Many times I have seen men choose the balm over the burden; in their eyes, in that moment ere I carved their soul from them, I saw the choice made. Perhaps Christ shall judge such men but I do not, for I too have trembled beneath the weight and many times been surprised I did not drop.

This time I rose, I think, through no prowess of my own but that granted by this one and abiding thought: *if I perish here, never again shall I see Walpurga* (and beneath it, like rot beneath gilding, this other thought: *never shall I know her betrayal, and its extent*).

Yet rise I did, all at once like a wrestler, raising my sword and parrying the Beast's downward bite, shedding its fangs like water off a roof. Its snout thudded to the earth and I thrust my own hand into my side and drew it forth wet and bloody as an infant unhomed from its mother's belly and I rubbed my own humor upon my sword and spoke aloud the *luceo non uro,* which is a prayer of dread and a psalm of war. Pain wrenched me as I chanted—fishhooks, pulling loose the knitting of my veins—and my blood flowed up and over my blade and by Christ and Iophiel, it *burned.*

I hewed at the Beast and where my blade alit, a black flame flared. Blood steamed forth like incense upon an altar. The Beast cried out and fled across the bridge of swords, its hooves aclamor and its gore smoking behind it like the tail of some outflung fragment of the heavens, mournful of its fall. Almost I pursued it, for that red and loving thirst was upon me, that holy zeal for the blood and the flesh which is gift and curse in equal measure.

But then I saw Prospero draped across a stone, his lifesblood haloed around him, and the flame of Iophiel snuffed itself from my blade. In the sudden dark, I limped towards him.

"Ah, sweet Belial," he whispered through a beard of blood, his voice the ratchet of the wheel upon a gallows. He pawed at his ruined self. "Blow wind, come wrack, at least I die with harness on my back."

He chuckled and coughed and was still. His eyes still moved however, and it was the Beast they hunted. I stared at him, and thought—very briefly—of many things.

Then, I drew from my belt the silver skull. My hands shook as I grubbed free that final Flesh and placed it within Prospero's mouth. I dribbled the dregs of the Blood onto his tongue. He coughed and sputtered and shuddered like a man undone as I heaved him onto my shoulders and carried him on, on, onward to the bridge of swords.

The first step upon that bridge near ended us both. The bridge was itself a blade of blades and where it touched, it cut. Already my wounds bled freely—both those inflicted upon me and those I rendered myself (for the Lord is jealous of His fire, even to we his chosen knights, and yea, only blood may pay for blood). I stepped forward and slipped on my own vital humor and fell and could not rise. My vision swam. My legs wobbled. My breath clattered in my throat like bones tossed down a barrow. I could not rise.

Across the bridge, the Beast paced and fretted at its wounds and lashed its tail and stared with eyes of balefire but it did not close. Above it, near as Death's own shadow, beckoned the Tower, an edifice out of those old times ere the splintering of the world and its native covenants, itself unworn and unconquered and bright at its peak with the untrammeled flame of eons. I saw it and was in my heart comforted for indeed it was as the Book must say: 'shall men seek death, and not find it; and shall desire to die, and death shall flee from them.'

I bled. Time passed. I bled more.

Something jabbed into my cheek. Almost I bit at it before I recognized it for a finger, and a man's.

"Belial," Prospero said, "liest thou upon my leg."

I did not laugh—I lacked the breath. Instead I crawled, an ant upon the earth, one clawing hand at a time, and thereby removed myself from my brother's limb. He stood then, a knight of rags, and his wounds staunched themselves before my eyes and in his gaze a strength like thunder dwelt. He reached out his hand and I grasped it and he hauled me up and staggered with my weight. I caught him and staggered likewise and he caught me and together, like some ungainly beast whelped beneath an errant star, all limbs and coltish joint, we stumbled forward, forward, across the bridge.

We reached its end, less knights and more liches carved bloody from the earth. Prospero's axe lay elsewhere, sundered by his fall. My sword, blood blackened to its blade, dragged upon the ground. Prospero clawed his misericorde from his belt. I leaned against him. The Beast regarded us, and in the slits of its eyes I saw reflected no hate nor malice but only that idiot, writhing hunger which alone of all other qualities is proof of inalienable divinity.

I crossed myself and Prospero coughed scarlet smoke. His eyes smoldered like steel set to anvil, stoked by the smithy's hammer until it were red and malleable and poison to the man but for his tonging iron.

"Smitest thou on the sinister," he said, "and allow me plucketh him upon the dexter and by such medicine shall we excuse our injuries and yea, now at long last make good on our rebel thunder."

Hearing him, I knew he was no longer my brother—and yet, would ever be. I smiled (for such a man must do, when there is nothing left). Sputum reddened my beard. The Beast, as if in preparation for our charge, limped backwards, towards the Tower. Never did its eyes leave us.

"Count of three," I said, "we charge."

But Prospero cried out, "Father! Thou tyrant! Thou flea!" and rushed forth and I towed in his wake as thunder staggers after lightning and before us, as if in answer to the tremble of our steps, the air itself thrummed and bulged and was like a pustule brimmed to its uttermost with rank humors of the flesh. We stumbled to a halt and watched it—wary as pilgrims in the desert for some fresh and sunlit hell—and I saw the Beast watched with us, its eyes anchored to that roiled air as if it were of one covenant with us, agonied and bloodied by the long, green twilight. But then the air trembled and swelled and was by its own self burst, and my eyes swept themselves from the Beast.

A gravewind roiled over us, sweet and salty and earthy by turns, and then a brume of brimstone sulfured us and we stepped back gagging, and emerald smoke fogged forth from a hole in the world. My eyes lidded themselves in rosary against that foul breath and when again they unsealed, I saw Walpurga.

She sat astride a destrier within that hole as though within a donjon's doorway, its edges ragged with flame, her one hand outstretched and smoking and trembling as though held against a great weight.

"Hieronymus," she said, and tears silvered her eyes.

Three strides (three stumbles) and I was upon her.

We kissed. Her lips came away bloody.

"We must away," she said, her voice strained, the tendons stark upon her neck. "The gate shall not hold."

Nearer to her now I saw the fresh scars runing her face and the burnt edges of her purple gown and the circlet of silver on her brow and the clawmarks tattooing her steed—who beneath them all was indeed young Iscariot—and behind her, tattered as myself and with eyes dull-lit by their rousing flames, dead knights atop dead steeds arrayed themselves in conroi.

Behind us, the Beast roared as though it was the sun itself hailing in the bloodstained day and I kissed her again and nodded and turned towards Prospero. But already, he was past me.

I held up my sword, for he declaimed now in a foreign tongue with a voice of fire and his eyes were not the eyes of Man and cradled in them no memory of brother or sister but shone only with blood and the promise of blood. Walpurga saw him and made a noise in her throat and I stood before her and leaned against her and felt her hand upon my back. But then Prospero dropped his dagger and held out his hand to a lich-knight and it matched its gaze to his own and what message their lights exchanged I cannot say.

A moment passed unspoken and then the lich-knight, as though in obeisance to its appointed lord, stepped down from its seat atop its destrier—which was a one-eyed thing, half its teeth laid bare and yellow to the moaning wind—and held out its hands, that Prospero might be mounted. He did so and once seated brandished his left arm and another lich came forth and strapped to that bloody limb a shield of unblazoned sable. He stretched out his right hand and a lich slapped into it a lance of pale ash, and then Prospero rode back, back into the glare of day.

The Beast reared upon its hind hooves and spread its foreclaws and howled its bitter accolade. Yet, Prospero did not halt his course. Blood flowed from him in rivers and in streams and in great, bright tears, as though his soul itself wept its own anointing. He tottered in his seat and I feared he might fall then and there and lay dead upon that foreign dust. But then he steadied himself and stood in his stirrups and the Tower's beam glanced from his plate and he breathed out and there was no smoke. Then he held high his lance in salute of the Beast and of God the Father and of other fathers who were, perhaps, more distant than Man may say.

Three times, he rode around us. Three times, he cried:

"Death!"

"Death!"

"Death!"